Nothing

Also by K. A. Last

Fiction

Sacrifice – A Fall For Me Prequel
(The Tate Chronicles, #0.5)
Bound (The Tate Chronicles, #0.6)
Fall For Me (The Tate Chronicles, #1)
Fight For Me (The Tate Chronicles, #2)
Die For Me (The Tate Chronicles, #3)
Immagica
The Lovely Dark
Something (All the Things: part one)
Nothing (All the Things: part two)
Everything (All the Things: part three)

Non-fiction

The Tate Chronicles Notebook
Immagica Notebook
A Novel Idea! Colouring Journal for Writers

Nothing

All the Things: part two

K. A. LAST

www.kalastbooks.com.au

K. A. Last
kalast@kalastbooks.com.au
www.kalastbooks.com.au

ISBN: 978-0-6480257-4-0

Formatting and cover design by KILA Designs
www.kiladesigns.com.au
Cover images: ©bigstockphoto.com

Editing by Lauren Clarke Editing
www.laurenclarkeediting.com

For every girl who has ever had her heart broken.

Contents

Veronica was wrong

For a moment I stand there, frozen. I can't believe what I've just heard.

Levi White asked me to the formal on a *dare*.

I twist my fingers together in an angry knot. I should confront him. Part of me wants to, but the other part wants to get the hell out of here. Levi and his mates have something else in store for me, and I have no idea what it is.

"Don't forget about the money," Jarred says.

Money? My back stiffens, and I wrap my arms around myself. Money for what?

"You'll get it," Levi says.

Geoff sniggers. "Hopefully Katie puts out for you. Might make it worth it."

Put out for him?

Cold washes through me, and I break out in a sweat. I grip my stomach as it fills with a sick feeling. I don't know whether to be upset or angry. Why would he agree to do something like this?

I need to get out of here.

But I'm at the top of the tallest tower in Sydney, and I can't move.

Levi comes around the corner and stops under the arch. Our gazes meet, and I'm trying so hard to hold it together. My eyes are hot, and I don't want to cry, but tears spill onto my cheeks anyway. I blink and squeeze my eyes shut, hoping that when I open them, Levi won't be standing there.

He is.

"Katie." He takes a step towards me, his hand out to touch my arm.

I back away and shake my head. "Don't." My lip trembles and I suck it between my teeth.

"What's wrong?" He frowns and drops his arm.

"Really? You're asking me what's wrong?"

Geoff and Jarred come into view behind Levi, and I want to punch both of them in their faces.

"Hey, Katie. Having a good night?" Geoff asks.

I puff out a breath, unable to breathe properly because I'm so mad.

I clench my teeth and stare at Levi. "Truth or dare?"

He raises his eyebrows. "You want to play now?"

"Isn't that how it works?" I ask. "Doesn't your stupid game go everywhere with you and your bunch of ... jerks?"

"How about we save it for the after-party?" Levi runs a hand through his hair and instead of getting butterflies,

I want to rip it off his head.

"What? You don't want to play now? Okay then. How about you, Geoff? Truth or dare?"

"Truth," he says without hesitating.

I take a deep breath. "Did someone dare Levi to ask me to the formal?"

Geoff's smile turns into a smirk. "Yes."

"And did they also bet that he'd get me to sleep with him?"

"You only get one question," Jarred says. "Now it's Geoff's turn."

"Fuck you." I glare at Levi but aim my words at all of them.

"That was the point," Geoff says, grinning.

I turn and run.

I flee across the dance floor, pushing my way past the moving bodies until I break through the other side. Bypassing the main bathrooms, I hug the curved wall of the restaurant and head for the second set, where it's quieter. The door slams open as I enter. A girl I've never really spoken to stands at the sink, touching up her lipstick. She takes one look at me and leaves.

I stop in the middle of the room, staring at my reflection in the large mirror. My eyes are red and puffy, and mascara has run onto my cheeks. I try to hold in the sobs, but I can't. My shoulders heave as I suck in breaths, and my throat goes dry. My brain is telling me to calm down, but my heart and body have other ideas.

Why did Levi have to be such an idiot?

There are three stalls. The first has an *out of order* sign stuck to the door. I push it open and go in, locking myself inside. I sit on the closed toilet lid and cry harder than I ever have before. It's like the pieces of my heart are pouring out with every breath, and falling onto the bathroom floor. I thought Levi and I were working towards something really special, but what we have is nothing.

The bathroom door squeals as someone opens it, and I hold my breath. I don't want anyone to see me like this. To know I'm this upset. I can't let them think they've gotten to me.

A girl giggles. "Shouldn't we check if anyone's in here?"

I recognise Veronica's voice, and I lift my legs to hug my knees to my chest, hoping she and whoever she's with won't discover me.

"Is there anyone in here?" Geoff's voice echoes off the tiles.

What is Veronica doing with Geoff?

I hold my breath.

"Check the stalls," Veronica says.

A door bangs against the stall wall beside me. Another bang. I imagine Geoff looking in the cubicles, and I'm glad there's the *out of order* sign on the door to my hiding place.

"Don't worry. No one's here," Geoff says. "We won't be long."

Veronica giggles again. They both make noises I don't want to hear. *They're making out in the girls' bathroom.* Could they have picked a more disgusting place? I press my palms to my ears, and put my forehead on my knees, waiting for it all to end.

Geoff groans. Feet shuffle along the floor.

"Ouch!" Veronica says.

Nothing

I take my hands away from my ears.

"Come on," Geoff says.

"Cut it out. You're hurting me."

What is he doing to her?

"You want it."

"No. I don't. Geoff, stop it."

"You do. You want it bad."

They don't talk for about ten seconds but it feels like ten hours.

"Stop, please." Veronica's voice is quieter now. She sniffles. "Please."

I get off the toilet as quietly as I can and put my eye to the crack at the edge of the stall door.

Geoff has Veronica pressed against the tiled wall. He's gripping her small wrists with one hand and has them pinned above her head. His other hand is under her dress. She struggles, then turns her head to the side away from the mirror, and closes her eyes.

I step away from the crack in the door and stand still, my hand on the lock.

What a dick.

As much as I don't like Veronica, I can't stay in here and let this happen. I would hope if I were ever in a situation like this that someone would help me.

Veronica sniffles again.

"Don't cry," Geoff says. "You love putting out."

I'm going to kill him.

Exactly what I'm going to do I'm not sure; I can't think that far ahead. Maybe my presence will be enough to stop what's happening. I look around the stall. There's a plastic toilet brush behind the bowl next to the sanitary bin. I lean over and grab it. It's not much of a weapon, but I'm going for surprise not grunt.

I turn the lock slowly with my other hand. The door creaks as I open it and I stop, my breath catching in my throat. I peek through and my gaze locks with Veronica's. I put a finger to my lips. Her eyes are glassy. She closes them and whimpers.

I creep out of the stall, my fingers curled tightly around the handle of the toilet brush, making them ache. I edge my way towards Geoff. Veronica struggles, as if my presence has given her another burst of strength over submission. He grips her hands tighter and slams her against the wall, making her cry out.

I'm paralysed. All I need to do is say something and this will stop, but I'm frozen.

Come on, Katie. Do something.

"Get off her," I say.

Geoff stops and looks over his shoulder. I raise the toilet brush.

"What are you going to do with that?" Geoff laughs. *He's drunk.*

He's moved away from Veronica enough for her to put her legs together. In a quick motion, she brings her knee up into his groin as I whack him over the head with the brush. He lets out a strangled cry, but it's not from being hit with my inadequate weapon.

Geoff lets go of Veronica's wrists and clutches himself, squeezing his eyes closed. She shoves him away and he stumbles across the floor.

I circle around Geoff so I can get between him and Veronica.

"Get out," I say.

"Or what?"

I shake my head. "Did someone dare you to do this? Is it part of your sick and twisted game?"

"You should back off, Katie. You'll pay for this," Geoff says.

"Don't threaten me." I stand as tall as I can. "I don't have anything to lose. You, on the other hand …"

Geoff straightens and backs towards the door, glaring at us. I raise the toilet brush, and my eyebrows, and give him the meanest look I can.

"Truth or dare, Katie." Geoff opens the door, and the noise of the music wafts into the bathroom as he leaves.

When he's gone, Veronica lets out a shrill laugh. "I can't believe you hit him with a toilet brush."

I stare at the plastic makeshift weapon in my hand. "It didn't work very well. Your knee was more effective."

Veronica laughs again, then slides down the wall until she's sitting on the floor. The laughter turns to sobs, and she puts a hand over her mouth as she cries. I push the stall door open, tossing the brush into the corner, and sit next to her, not caring if the floor will dirty my dress. I don't like her, and we're definitely not friends, but she needs someone right now, and if that someone has to be me, then so be it. Compared to what Veronica just went through, my problems are insignificant. Yes, Levi has hurt me—more than once—but he's never forced himself on me.

Veronica said stop. Geoff ignored that, and that's not okay.

Veronica wipes her nose with the back of her hand. I

get up to grab some tissues from the box on the vanity and offer them to her. I sit beside her again, wondering what to do next. I can't leave her, and I certainly don't want to go back out to the formal.

"Why are you being nice to me?" Veronica wipes her eyes.

"No one deserves something like this happening to them," I say. "Are you ... did he ...?" I can't say the words.

She shakes her head. "It could've been worse. You stopped him."

"You need to report him."

"I need to forget this ever happened."

"Have you ever ... you know ... done ... it?"

"You mean sex?" Veronica asks. "Have I had sex?"

"Have you?"

"Jarred has told everyone we have. Geoff will tell everyone we did. It's all part of the game."

"Isn't it supposed to be about truth?"

Veronica laughs, but it's not a happy sound. "It hasn't been about truth for a long time. Now it's all about doing the most damage."

"That's ... It's a stupid game."

Veronica gets up and goes to the vanity, leaning over one of the basins that line the wall. She wets a tissue and gets to work cleaning the mascara and eyeliner that has run under her eyes.

I stay on the floor, the emotion of the night overwhelming me. I squeeze my eyes closed and let the tears fall, feeling relief wash over me as I stop fighting. I came in here to grieve my own loss, and instead I have had to be the strong one. I'm tired of being strong. Years of hurt and pain gush out of me, and I don't care that Veronica is here to see it.

Veronica sits next to me again, and this time it's her turn to offer me a tissue.

"Why are *you* crying?" she asks. "Isn't your life perfect now with Levi?"

"It would be if he actually wanted to be with me," I say.

"Trust me, he does."

"Enough to ask me to the formal on a dare?" I look at Veronica, and her mouth opens then closes again. *Guilty.* "Yeah, I found out about that."

Veronica shakes her head and smiles. "Are you this stupid all the time?"

"I think I should be offended."

"Why do you think Levi has never had a girlfriend?"

"Yes, he has."

"Not really," she says. "Sure, he's made out with people, but he's never had a serious relationship. It's always been you, Katie."

"So, he took a dare that forced him to ask me to the formal, and said he had to sleep with me. Oh, and there's money involved with that second part." I laugh. "That's got love written all over it."

"He *is* in love with you. He just never wanted to admit it."

"Can't half guess why." I stare at my hands and wrap the skirt of my dress around my finger. The urge to rip it to shreds washes over me. Maybe I'll burn it when I get home.

"You need to ask him why he agreed to do the dare in the first place."

"I don't want to talk to him ever again."

We go quiet for a few seconds, then Veronica laughs.

"What's so funny?"

"This." Veronica motions between us. "Us ... talking. Never thought I'd see the day." She stares at me, and then her smile falls away. "Thank you."

"For what? Hitting Geoff with a toilet brush?"

She chuckles. "I'm serious, Katie. If you weren't here ..."

"Report him."

Veronica gets to her feet. "It won't make a difference."

"Does Jarred know?"

"Stop trying to fix my problems."

The door bursts open, and Karen spills into the bathroom. She stops dead, and stares at Veronica and me. We must be a sight: both of us with red, puffy faces, and panda eyes. Veronica's dress has a rip in the skirt. She grabs one of the straps that's fallen off her shoulder and puts it back in place.

"What happened? What did you do to her?" Karen comes towards Veronica.

I jump up and stand between them. "Don't, Karen. She didn't do anything. Geoff attacked her."

"She probably asked for it."

"You'd think that, wouldn't you?" Veronica says.

"If the shoe fits." Karen folds her arms and glares.

"Karen, don't be a bitch," I say.

She turns her glare on me. "Okay, one: what did you just call me? And two: you're defending her?"

I wrap my arms around my stomach to stop myself falling apart again. "Geoff tried to ... he assaulted her. And I stopped him."

Nothing

"Would you shut up, Katie," Veronica says. "It was nothing."

Karen looks Veronica up and down, her gaze travelling over her torn dress. "Are you okay?" she finally asks.

"What do you care?" Veronica pushes past us to the basin and finishes fixing her makeup.

"I'm sorry. I thought you were hurting Katie."

Veronica puts her compact down and leans on the edge of the sink. She drops her head, and her shoulders shake. "Please don't tell anyone about this."

"We won't." I put a hand on her shoulder.

She stands up straight and blinks rapidly. "Thanks."

Veronica goes to the door and Karen takes a few steps with her. "You want us to come out with you?"

Veronica shakes her head and opens the door. "You need to stay with Katie. She has her own problems to deal with."

Karen and I watch the door close, and I wish Veronica was wrong.

2

My heart, again

I fill Karen in on everything that's happened since I left her to find Levi. She listens without interrupting until I'm finished. Then she goes into attack mode.

"I'm going to kill him. And Geoff, for good measure."

"Please, don't do anything," I say. "I don't want to talk to Levi. I don't even want to look at him."

"Doesn't mean I can't give him what for."

I stare at Karen and suck my bottom lip between my teeth. "Just … keep him away from me for the rest of the night."

She sighs. "Okay, but I can't promise I won't do anything after we get out of here."

We leave the bathroom and go back to the main room. As we pass the dance floor, Stacey grabs my hand and pulls me into the throng. We move to the centre of the crowd, masked by the mass of bodies moving around us. Maybe more dancing is exactly what I need. It's time to really let my hair down.

I glance at Karen and she smiles, moving her hips to the beat. Stacey and Jessica complete our little circle, and everywhere I look people are having fun. Everyone on the dance floor has taken their inhibitions and thrown them in the air. I raise my arms above my head and let loose.

"You, me, dancing. Every weekend from now on," Karen yells in my ear.

The music slows, and so do we, swaying to the beat. I tilt my head back and close my eyes, trying to immerse myself in this moment, and think about nothing else.

A hand slips around my waist. "I've been looking for you." Levi's breath tickles my ear. He smells like sweaty aftershave and alcohol.

How dare he touch me? I turn to face him, and shove his arms away at the same time.

I slap him.

Levi presses a hand to his cheek, but I don't stick around to hear what he has to say. I storm off the dance floor, pushing my way through the crowd. But where am I going to go? We can't leave the tower until the night is officially over. I'm stuck up here, looking out over the city lights. An immense feeling of claustrophobia engulfs me.

"Katie, wait," Levi says, but I don't stop.

When I reach the arch leading into the foyer he grabs my arm, and I spin to face him. "Don't touch me."

"Please, let me explain."

"What is there to explain, Levi? You asked me to the

formal on a dare."

"It's not what you think—"

"Oh, really? So what's the money for? Did they dare you to sleep with me, too? You really are a jerk."

"Come on. Don't be angry," he says.

I take a step towards him. He smiles a lopsided, goofy grin, and I smell the booze on his breath. He probably thinks he looks sexy. I think he looks like a drunken idiot.

"Never, in a million years, will I let you touch me again."

Levi frowns and sways on his feet. "It's not—"

"Oh please. Tell me what I *should* think, because I'm dying to hear your lame excuse."

"I was protecting you."

"From what?" I yell. "The only thing I need protection from is you."

"I can explain."

I shake my head and laugh. "No, Levi, you can't charm yourself out of this one. Tell me, how much is sex with me actually worth?"

Levi opens and closes his mouth a few times before clamping it shut.

I turn to go back into the restaurant and freeze. We have an audience. A small group of formal goers have come over to see what's happening. Karen stands at the front, Jessica and Stacey on either side of her. Veronica is scowling, which isn't surprising. She turns and goes back towards the tables. I'm not the only one having a crappy night.

"You're such a dick, Levi," Karen says. "And your friends are, too."

14

"Katie, I'm sorry," Levi says.

"It's a bit late for sorry." I find Geoff and Jarred's faces in the small crowd.

I shake my head and turn my back on Levi, moving through the people to go to our table. I slide into the chair beside Veronica and stare at the lights with her. Karen, Jessica, and Stacey sit with us. None of us talk. No one seems in the mood.

After a while, Veronica looks around as if she's just noticed us sitting with her. For once, she doesn't make a snide or bitchy remark. Instead, she smiles, and the five of us watch the lights, waiting until we can get out of here.

The music stops, and I look around the room. Britney Owens, our vice-captain, takes the stage and grabs the microphone.

"It's time," she says in a sing-song voice. "Everyone has voted and we've tallied the results. Gather around to celebrate the crowning of your king and queen."

Karen rolls her eyes, and I laugh at her expression. We pretty much know Veronica will win queen. She has so many supporters. And those who don't like her are too afraid not to vote for her.

Everyone moves towards the stage except us. We're all over tonight, and I, for one, do not care who gets crowned.

"Are you ready?" Britney asks. A few people shout out and wolf whistle. "Please put your hands together for this year's queen, Veronica Porter."

The room erupts into applause, but Veronica doesn't look overly excited about winning. She stands from her seat, and makes her way to the stage using slow steps.

Britney places the crown on Veronica's head, and she adjusts it before taking the microphone.

"I'm honoured, of course," Veronica says, putting on her sweet voice. "And we can celebrate at the after-party." She puts one hand in the air and gives a loud whoop.

Everyone follows suit, and starts clapping and whistling.

"Okay, settle down everyone," Britney says. "Now it's time to announce our king, who is none other than our very own school captain, Levi White."

The room erupts again. I'm not surprised he was voted in. I even voted for him. I spot Levi over the other side of the room, walking around the edge of the crowd towards the stage. Veronica's line of sight follows him as he approaches. Then she laughs, and more laughter bursts from the front, but I can't see what's going on because I'm sitting.

"I'm okay," Levi says when he's up on the stage. He sways a bit.

Whispers move through the students, and I put my face in my hands.

"He's drunk," I say. "This should be good."

"Is everyone having a good time?" Levi asks. More whoops and whistles. "Thank you for voting for me. I'd like to say I'm happy to be standing here beside Ronnie ..." He puts an arm around her and pulls her close. "... but I'm not. I should be standing here with Katie."

"Oh no," I say, peeking through my fingers. "He isn't ..."

Karen jumps up and races over to the music station, whispering in the DJ's ear.

Levi stumbles forward. "Katie, I'm sorry ..."

Nothing

Everyone in the room stops talking.

I sit back in my chair and let my eyes go blurry. This isn't happening.

Seconds later, music blares from the speakers once again. Britney grabs the microphone from Levi, and pushes him and Veronica onto the dance floor for the king and queen's dance.

I take a deep breath, willing the last hour of the formal to go as fast as possible.

As soon as we can, Karen, Jessica, Stacey, and I get the hell out of there. We're the first ones in the lift. We have no plans of going to the after-party, and we grab the first taxi we can find. It takes us all the way to my place, and none of us talk much on the way home. Jessica and Stacey walk the few houses down to Jessica's place before Karen and I go inside. I put on my bravest face, giving Mum, Dad, and Daniel a quick rundown of the night and how *great* it was.

"How was the food?" Daniel asks.

I shrug. "Okay, I guess." I didn't eat much.

"And the dancing?" Mum asks.

"Yeah, we did some of that." Karen smiles.

I think back to how good it felt to move in time with the music, but the feeling of happiness is crushed by the memories of what happened with Levi and Veronica.

"The best part was the view," I say, pretending there's nothing wrong.

"I'm glad you had a good time," Mum says.

Dad sits at the kitchen table and sips a cup of coffee. "I hope the boys behaved."

"Um ... yeah. They were fine." I fake a yawn. "We

should go and get all this stuff off."

"Yes," Karen says. "Can't sleep in our makeup."

"I'm going to bed, too," Daniel says. "Waiting up for you two is tiring work."

Everyone heads up the stairs and goes their separate ways. The hall echoes with 'good night' as we close our doors.

Once Karen and I are in my room, everything changes, and my mood comes crashing down again. I've managed to mostly hold it together, but I can't contain it anymore.

I flop onto my bed and push my face into my pillow, sobbing. All my heartache pours out, soaking the pillowcase and filling it with sorrow. Karen's weight dips the bed as she sits beside me. She rubs my back, but doesn't speak, and I'm so grateful for her presence and her silence.

"Come on. Let's get you out of this dress," she says when my sobs subside.

She helps me up and unzips me. I stand in the middle of my room, numb. All my emotion is gone, and in its place is nothing. I'm an empty shell, and I want to stay like this, not feeling, because emptiness is better than pain.

Karen helps me into my PJs. She brushes my hair and cleans the makeup off my face with some cleansing wipes.

I stare at my dress pooled on the floor. It's such a pretty dress, but now I hate it. I pull it onto my lap and run my hand over the bodice, brushing my fingertips over the embroidery on the waistband.

"Why did he do this to me?" I whisper.

Karen squeezes my arm. "Because he's an idiot."

Nothing

My fingers find the loops in the embroidery and I dig them in. Then I pull as hard as I can. The fabric rips, and I tear at it until the dress is a mess of fabric on my knees. Karen doesn't try to stop me. Hot tears sting my eyes. I throw the dress across the room.

Karen wraps her arms around me and I sob into her shoulder. "It isn't fair."

"Shhh, I know." She strokes my hair.

I get under the covers and bury my face in my pillow. Karen pulls the trundle out from under my bed, and busies herself with making up the mattress with the sheets Mum has left on my desk. I lie and watch as she works in silence. She takes her own dress off and changes into her PJs before slipping out the door to go to the bathroom.

I must fall asleep because the next thing I hear is tapping on my window. Karen is snoring softly on the trundle beside me. She has her head under her pillow and I smile. She's always slept like that. She never could sleep with it around the right way. Light from the street shines through the gap in the curtains.

The tapping sounds again.

I get out of bed, careful not to step on Karen, and go to the window seat. When I part the curtains Levi is staring at me, and I hope he can see the hurt in my eyes. I hope he can see it down to my soul.

What he's done has broken me.

I want to open the window and let him climb in like he has so many times before. But there is no room for him in my life anymore. He has reduced us to nothing.

Before I can stop myself I push the bottom sash of the

window up.

"Can we talk?" Levi asks. His breath smells like bourbon.

"There's nothing to talk about."

"Come on, Katie. Please let me explain."

"You're drunk. Again. That's explanation enough."

"You need to hear the truth."

I grit my teeth. "The truth is that you never wanted to be with me in the first place. You asked me out because one of your stupid friends dared you to, and there's money involved. I think all of that is pretty self-explanatory."

He shakes his head. "It's not like that." His foot slips on the roof, and he grabs the windowsill.

I kneel on the window seat and wait for him to adjust his footing. Then I lean in close. He smiles, and I bet he thinks I'm going to kiss him.

In a harsh whisper I say, "If you don't get off my roof right now, so help me God, Levi, I will push you off."

"Katie—"

"No. You're drunk. Get. Down. I never want to see you again."

He presses his lips together and moves away from the window. I pull the sash closed, turn the lock, and draw the curtains. I step over Karen who has slept through our entire encounter, her head still under her pillow.

I climb back under my covers and pull them to my chin, vowing never to let Levi into my room, or my heart, again.

Sorry won't fix anything

*A*ttendance at school after the formal is optional, and I opt not to go. I lie in bed and stare at the ceiling, trying not to remember what happened. At least I have a two week break now, and I don't have to leave the house for days if I don't want to. I'll be able to study for HSC exams, which start in three weeks.

Who am I kidding? All I can think about is Levi.

He's broken my heart in the worst way possible, and now I'm lost. I got my hopes up about a future together. Not a get-married-and-have-kids kind of future, but one where we both went off to uni, maybe the same one, and hung out for a while.

I don't know what uni I'll be attending yet. I won't find out until final results are released in December, and acceptance letters start to arrive. If I get my first choice,

Mum and Dad aren't going to be happy. I haven't even told them I applied for a fine arts degree. As I stare at my ceiling, counting the faded glow-in-the-dark stars, I realise that right now I don't care anyway. I'm as dull as the stars have become over the years, blending in with the white paint. An endless expanse of nothingness. And the longer I stare, the bigger it gets.

I roll onto my side and stare down at Karen. She stretches on the trundle and blinks the sleep from her eyes.

"Hey," I say.

"Hey. New day. Has to be better than the last."

I force a smile.

We get up and take turns in the shower before heading downstairs for some breakfast. Daniel is at the stove, flipping pancakes.

"Where's my brother, and what have you done to him?" I ask.

He smiles. "Good morning, sleepyheads. I felt like pancakes. Want some?"

"Why aren't you at work?" I ask.

"First Friday off in ages." Daniel slides a pancake onto a plate, and pours the next lot of batter into the pan. "Grab some plates and cutlery, would you?"

Mum races down the stairs, dressed for work. She kisses me on the cheek. "Morning, girls."

"It's nine-thirty. Why are you still here?" I ask, taking three plates from the cupboard and setting them on the kitchen bench.

"Late meeting." Mum pours herself a coffee and takes a quick sip. "Will you be home for dinner? Dad thought we could order Thai."

"Sure," I say, but my heart sinks at the mention of Thai food.

The last time I ate it was with Levi at the park. It's a nice memory, but thinking about him makes me think about what he's done, especially since that's the night he asked me to go to the formal with him. I've successfully not thought about him for at least ten minutes. Now I can't stop thinking about him, again.

"I'll be home around five. Stay out of trouble," Mum says before putting her mostly untouched cup in the sink and heading for the door.

"Never," Daniel says. "But we promise not to burn the house down."

I grab some cutlery then Karen and I sit at the counter, and Daniel puts a plate between us. Steam rises from the stack of pancakes, and we take one each. I smother mine in maple syrup and dive in. Daniel turns the stove off and puts the pan in the sink.

He leans on the bench and stares at me. "Okay, spill. What's the matter?"

"Nothing." I take a big bite so I don't have to talk.

"You can't fool me, Katie. Something's up. What happened last night?"

"How do you do that?" I ask.

"Do what?" Daniel shrugs.

"Know me so well." I stab my pancake with my fork.

"You're my little sister. It's my job."

"Levi was dared to have sex with Katie," Karen blurts.

"What?" Daniel asks.

I drop my fork onto my plate and glare at Karen. "Why did you tell him that?"

"It's Daniel." She shrugs. "Maybe he can beat him up."

I glare at my brother. "You are not going to beat him up."

"I am *so* going to beat him up."

"I didn't *actually* have sex with him," I say. "And the original dare was to take me to the formal."

Daniel stomps out of the kitchen towards the front door. I roll my eyes at Karen and chase after him. He's already on the front lawn before I make it outside. Daniel pounds on Levi's front door with a closed fist. I hope he won't hit Levi as hard as he's hitting the wood. Or hit him at all. As mad as I am, I've already slapped him once, and it didn't make me feel any better.

As I reach the steps to Levi's house, Yvonne opens the door, surprise masking her face.

"Where is he?" Daniel says before she can open her mouth.

"Sorry," I say, puffing. "Daniel's looking for Levi. Is he home?"

"No. I'm afraid I haven't seen him yet." She frowns. "I thought he'd come home with you, so I'm not sure where he is."

"His car is here," Daniel says. "He must be home."

"Daniel, calm down." I put a hand on his arm.

"What's this about? Is everything okay?" Yvonne looks between the both of us. "Did something happen, Katie?"

My brother opens and closes his fists a few times. "I want to talk to him about something."

"Everything's fine. We can talk to Levi later." I tug Daniel's arm. "We should go."

Daniel presses his lips together, then nods and turns

to walk down the steps. I go to follow, but Yvonne reaches out and touches my shoulder.

"Are you sure everything's okay, sweetie?" she asks.

"You coming, Katie?" Daniel calls over his shoulder.

"In a minute," I reply. Yvonne and I watch my brother walk across our yards and go inside. I take a deep breath and turn back to Levi's mum. "I'm sure everything will be fine."

"Okay." She rubs my arm. "I'll tell Levi you were looking for him?"

"Oh no, it's fine. Don't worry about it." I offer her a smile before descending the steps and walking towards home.

The door to Levi's house clicks closed, and I glance back at the empty veranda. I stop on the boundary of our two properties and look at Levi's car parked on the street. He put it there last night so the stretch Hummer could use the driveway.

I squint against the morning sun, and notice the car windows are partly down. Not just one, but all four. Slowly, I walk towards the BMW, and when I reach the passenger side, I bend to look in through the open part of the window.

Levi is asleep on the back seat.

His head rests at a funny angle on the armrest in the door. He has one leg bent at the knee leaning against the back of the seat, while the other hangs over the edge into the footwell. On the floor is a silver hip flask. My guess is it's empty.

I straighten and back away from the car.

"Katie?" Levi asks.

I stop and stare at him as he moves to a sitting position. He peers at me through the partially open window while the rest of his face is shielded by the tinted glass. Why did I come over here? I don't want to see him or talk to him.

I turn away. I get halfway to my front door before I hear the car door open and close, but I don't turn around.

"Katie," Levi says again.

I keep walking and reach the stairs. The soft thud of footsteps follows me.

"Katie, please." He grabs my arm and I yank it away, turning to face him.

"I should never have come out here."

"Why did you?"

"Daniel wants to punch you. Hard," I say. "I was going to stop him."

Levi clenches his jaw. "What did you tell him?

"You mean besides the fact you're a jerk, dickhead, and an arsehole who ripped my heart out, threw it on the floor, and then stomped on it?"

Levi winces.

"You better get out of here," Karen says through the screen door. "If Daniel sees you …"

"I'm not leaving until Katie hears me out," Levi says.

"You don't deserve to have her listen to you." Karen opens the door.

I move up the steps then stop. "Why were you in your car?"

"Why do you care?"

I scoff and shake my head. "I don't."

We stare at each other, and the longer we stand there the more the anger boils inside me. My eyes burn, but I don't feel like I'll cry. I cried enough tears last night to last me three lifetimes.

"I didn't want to go in and face Dad. Okay?" Levi says.

"Because you were drunk?"

He drops his gaze and stuffs his hands in his pockets. He's still wearing his suit pants and once white shirt.

"Dad … he's not—"

"I can't do this right now," I say. "To be honest, I don't care what you're going through. I don't care if you want to drown your sorrows in a bottle of booze. All I care about is forgetting you even exist. You made me fall in love with you, and now … we have nothing, Levi. You made me feel like I was nothing but a piece in your stupid game."

Karen is still holding the screen door open and I grip the handle, pulling it closed as I go inside.

"You're in love with me?" Levi asks.

I look back at him through the screen. "Not anymore." Then I slam the wooden door as hard as I can.

"Daniel?" I call out, moving past Karen.

"Kitchen," he says.

"Can you help me with something?" I sit at the kitchen counter.

He wipes the frypan over with a tea towel and sets it on the bench. "What would this something be?"

"I want to rip the trellis down."

"You want to what?" Karen asks. "Won't your parents be pissed?"

"I'm hoping they won't notice." I shrug.

"What? You think they're not going to miss the massive pink and green plant stuck to their house?" She puts her hands on her hips.

"I'm not sure, Katie," Daniel says. "Karen is right."

"Then I'll call Dad." I run upstairs and grab my phone from my desk before either of them can protest. I'm already talking to Dad before I make it back to the kitchen. "I think we need a change."

"But you love that bougainvillea," Dad says.

"Change is as good as a holiday." I slide onto a stool at the kitchen counter.

"Did something happen with Levi?" Dad asks.

I hesitate and look at Karen, even though she didn't hear the question. "What makes you think that?"

"Well, last time we pruned it because he was climbing in your window. Now you want it gone ... I'm thinking it might have something to do with you *not* wanting him to climb in your window."

"He doesn't do that anymore. And we pruned it because it scratches the house, remember?"

"Katie," Dad says in his best fatherly voice. "I wasn't born yesterday."

"And you didn't come down in the last shower either." I laugh, but it's bitter.

Dad is silent for a few heartbeats, then he asks, "Are you sure everything is okay?"

I wish people wouldn't ask that question. *No, I'm not sure if everything is okay. I'm not sure about anything.* "I'm fine, Dad," I eventually say.

"All right. If I come home and the bougainvillea isn't there, I won't be angry."

"Great."

"But I will be angry if something's happened and you're not okay."

Nothing

"Really, I'm fine. We just ... had a fight. It happens." I look at Karen and Daniel, and they both shake their heads.

"Boys, huh?" Dad laughs.

"Yeah. Bye, Dad." I end the call and set my phone on the counter. "Who's up for some bougainvillea butchering?"

"I guess we'll need the ladder, and a couple of butchering devices." Daniel smiles, puts the frypan in the cupboard, and heads for the back door. "I'll grab some tools and meet you girls out the front."

Karen looks at me and bursts out laughing.

"What's so funny?" I ask.

"This is not how I pictured us spending the first day of our break."

I follow her to the front door. "We don't exactly get a break. Remember those things called exams?"

"Yeah, whatever. You already made dux. Don't sweat it." Karen opens the door. "And we have your birthday to celebrate next week as well."

I groan. "You know I hate doing stuff for my birthday. And this year is worse because it's right before exams."

"You're turning eighteen! I'm making you do something."

I close the door, and we walk down the steps and around to the side of the house. Daniel is there and has set up a ladder. He's also laid two pairs of pruning shears and a garden saw on the ground.

"Looks like hard work." I pick up the garden saw.

"This was your idea." Daniel grabs a pair of shears and walks up the ladder a few steps. "Not mine."

"Daniel, tell her she has to do something for her eighteenth." Karen stands with one hand on her hip, looking up at my brother and shading her eyes with her other hand.

"Katie hates parties," Daniel says. He leans over and snips a branch off near the top of the bougainvillea.

I nod. "He's right. I do."

Karen sighs. "Fine. But we're going to talk about this later." She picks up the other pair of garden shears.

The three of us set to work, cutting and sawing at the branches of the bougainvillea. Some of them have really entwined themselves into the lattice, and it's hard work cutting them loose.

"Maybe we need the chainsaw," Daniel says.

Karen laughs. "Do you even know how to use one?"

"If it's too hard just cut all the branches that have flowers," I say.

"But there's so much pink." Karen snips another branch then stands back and stares at the pile we've made on the ground.

Daniel steps down a rung on the ladder. "Pass me the saw, Katie."

I hand it up to him and take the shears, attacking a lower branch while Daniel works on a higher one.

The lattice is attached to the house from around a metre off the ground. There are two panels side by side that reach up to the second storey, but it's the one on the right that gives access to the small section of roof outside my bedroom window. The main trunk of the plant grows up in front of the left panel, so I concentrate on untangling the limbs and leaves from the right one.

"Maybe we only have to cut half of it down," I say. "I want to get the right lattice panel off the wall."

"Are you making this up as you go along?" Daniel asks.

"Pretty much." I smile at him. "I don't want Levi climbing up to my room … ever again."

"That's nice to know," Levi says.

I spin around.

He's standing on his driveway, glaring at me.

Anger rises into my chest. Is *he* mad at *me*?

Daniel climbs down the ladder. "Get lost, Levi."

"I'd listen to him if I were you," Karen says. "He has a potential murder weapon in his hand."

"You're cutting down the bougainvillea?" Levi ignores Daniel and Karen.

I take a step towards Levi and adjust my grip on the garden shears. "Yes, we're cutting it down."

"Why? If you don't want me to climb it, I won't."

"You say when you're sober." I glare at him.

He folds his arms over his chest, and looks at the pile of cut branches on the ground then back at me. "Katie, can we please talk?"

"Oh, did you hear that?" Karen says. "He said please."

I shake my head. "No. I told you I don't want to talk to you."

Levi laughs, and I grit my teeth.

"Why are you laughing?" Karen asks. "Nothing about this is funny."

Levi rubs his face, and has one last chuckle into his hand before stopping. "It kinda is." He turns his stare on me again. "Katie, I'm trying to apologise, and I at least deserve to be able to give you an explanation."

I take a deep breath and say, "No. What you deserve

is to be treated the same way you've treated me. You ruined everything, and I will never forgive you."

"Cutting down the bougainvillea won't change anything," Levi says.

I clench my fingers around the handle of the garden shears. "And you think telling me you're sorry will? Sorry won't fix anything."

Second chance

Mum and Dad didn't say much about the bougainvillea. After Mum saw it, she gave me one of those 'I understand' kinds of looks. The ones only mums know how to give.

For the past few days I've thrown myself into study. It's the first week of the break, and if I was in any other year at school, I'd be off having fun with my friends and doing whatever. Just chilling out. But I have HSC exams starting the second week of term four, so even though I've officially finished school classes for like forever, I haven't finished school.

But, as much as I want to study today, and hide in my room away from the world, Karen won't let me.

She's taking me out for my birthday.

Yay.

I have never liked celebrating my birthday. Not because I'm a party pooper or anything, but because I don't see the point. We never had enough money for Daniel and me to receive presents that we didn't need or that weren't practical, so it took the fun out of it. Now, if Mum and Dad spend money on me it makes me feel guilty, not happy.

Okay, maybe I am a party pooper.

"We're hitting the shops," Karen says from the other end of the phone. "I have a surprise for you, and then I'm taking you out for hot chocolate."

"Great," I say. "I love surprises." *Not.*

"I'm picking you up in fifteen minutes, so be ready." Karen hangs up.

I stare at my screen. A surprise? This can't be good.

It's warm today, so I change into my favourite denim skirt and a pale blue singlet top with wide straps. I slip my feet into a pair of sandals, grab my phone and tote bag, and head downstairs, dumping my stuff at the front door.

"Happy birthday," Mum says when I come into the kitchen. There's a small present sitting on the bench.

Mum is busy making coffee and breakfast. I give her a kiss, grateful that she's going about her morning routine, and not making a fuss.

"Happy birthday, kiddo." Daniel kisses me on the cheek on his way through from the lounge.

"Neither of you working today?" I ask.

"I took the day off." Mum flicks the kettle on. "Thought I'd make your favourite breakfast for you."

"Toast and tea?" I raise my eyebrows. "I can do that."

"Nonsense. I've got this." Mum smiles and puts two pieces of bread in the toaster. I laugh, and her smile is infectious.

"I'm not rostered on today," Daniel says. "Open your present."

"Are you scheming with Karen? She said she has a surprise for me." I slide onto one of the stools at the kitchen bench and pick up the small box.

"She may know what's going on." Daniel laughs. "You'll love it."

"God help me," I mumble.

"This is the first part." My brother sits on the stool beside me, pointing to the box in my hand. "Open it."

I take a deep breath and turn the small present over in my hands a few times. It's wrapped in pretty purple paper with a white ribbon. I have no idea what's inside.

"Dad left early?" I ask, already knowing the answer.

"He looked in on you but you were sound asleep," Mum says. "He didn't want to wake you."

"I shouldn't open this until he gets home," I say.

"He won't mind," Daniel says. "Open the present!"

I raise my eyebrows but don't say anything else. I pull the end of the ribbon to undo the bow. Daniel leans on the bench, his eyes wide and a smile on his face. I take extra care not to rip the paper as I peel the sticky tape off, knowing that it's driving my brother crazy. Still, he doesn't say anything. But he leans closer when I remove the paper.

Underneath is a purple box with a lid. I take the lid off and there's white tissue paper inside.

"Oh, come on, you're killing me," Daniel says. "Hurry up."

I laugh, and take the tissue paper out. Something

metal falls onto the bench.

It's a key.

And I'm pretty sure it's the kind that starts a car.

I pick the key up and stare at the Toyota logo imprinted on the bow, running my thumb over it. The button that opens the locks hangs off a small keychain loop.

"Did you buy me a car?"

Daniel laughs. "You'll have to go and see."

"But … we can't afford for you to buy me a car." I look at Mum.

"It's okay, sweetie. We haven't bought you a car," she says.

Now I laugh. "Damn." But I smile as well. I look at the key again. "Is this your car key, Mum?"

She grins.

"Would you just …" Daniel shoves his fingers into his hair. "Go and look in the car!"

I get off the stool and go out the front door to the driveway. Mum's Toyota Camry is parked where it always is. The car doesn't look any different, and I wonder what on Earth my family has in store for me. I lean down and peer through the front driver's side window. There's another package on the front seat.

"Seriously, do you need help unlocking the car?" Daniel asks.

Mum laughs behind me.

A horn blares before I can answer, and I straighten to see Karen pulling up to the kerb. She turns her mum's car off and jumps out.

"Did you open it?" Karen asks. "Has she opened it?" She looks to Daniel and Mum.

Nothing

"She's taking her sweet time," Daniel says.

I poke my tongue out at him and press the button on the keyring. The door locks pop up. Daniel grabs the handle and pulls the door open. He looks more excited than I feel. Right now, I'm just confused.

Daniel pushes me into the car and I swipe the parcel off the front seat before sitting on it. The package isn't very big, about the size of a DL envelope, wrapped in the same pretty paper as the box. Daniel leans on the open car door while Mum and Karen peer at me through the window.

"Hurry up," Karen says. "This is torture!"

I smirk then unwrap the parcel, quickly this time. There's a card and an envelope. When I open the card I see straight away it's from Mum, Dad, and Daniel. Karen's eyes are wide and she's waving her hands around.

"Dear Katie," I read. "We can't believe our little girl is all grown up ..." Mum smiles when I glance at her. "You've worked so hard to get this far, and we wanted to reward you with something you'll hopefully never forget. Your surprise is in the envelope. We hope you love it."

I put the card on my lap and pick up the envelope, turning it over so I can tear it open. I pull out the contents. There's a folded piece of A4 paper, and another envelope that has *Love Daniel* written on the front. I rip it open and find one hundred and fifty dollars inside.

"It's not much," Daniel says. "But I saved it so you could have some spending money."

My mouth hangs open. "Spending money? For what?"

"Unfold the paper," Mum says, grinning.

I slip the money back into the smaller envelope and open the piece of paper. Printed on it are reservation details for two people at a hotel in Surfers Paradise. Seven nights in an ocean-view room, breakfast included. Written at the bottom in my father's sprawling handwriting are the words, *Love Mum and Dad*.

"Two weeks after exams, we're going on a road trip," Karen squeals.

I stare at the paper and my smile falters. How can they afford this? Staying anywhere on the Gold Coast during schoolies week isn't cheap. I fold the paper again and put everything back into the envelope, then get out of the car. Daniel steps back and I close the door.

"Before you say anything," Mum says, "don't worry about the cost. You work so hard, Katie. Your father and I want you to have this. Okay?"

I force a smile. "Sure, Mum. It's going to be great."

"I haven't given you my present yet," Karen says, handing me a small package.

I lean against Mum's car and open the card taped to the top of the carefully wrapped present, also in purple paper. It's from Karen and her parents. When I rip the paper off, I find a fuel card, a pen, and a beautiful leather-covered journal.

"Mum and Dad are paying for our fuel. We can take Mum's car," Karen says. "And I know you love to write in your journal, so I figured you'd want a special one for this trip."

"This is all really … great," I say.

"Well, don't get too excited." Daniel frowns.

"I'm sorry. I am. I just …"

Mum gives me a big hug. "I know, honey. But all I want you to focus on is having an amazing time."

Nothing

I bury my face in her hair and nod.

A door opens and Mum pulls away. I look over to Levi's place where he's coming down the front steps of his veranda. He stops on the path and our gazes meet. I do *not* want to see him today.

He presses his lips together. "Happy birthday, Katie."

I push off the car and don't reply, heading straight for my front door and not looking at him.

"Sorry, Levi," I hear Mum say. "I didn't raise her to be so rude."

Seconds later Mum, Daniel, and Karen are all in the foyer with me.

"You could've said thank you," Mum says.

"No," Karen says.

"Nope," Daniel agrees. "He deserves everything he gets."

"What's going on?" Mum folds her arms. "Dad told me you and Levi are fighting. Is it so bad between you two that you've lost your manners?"

"I don't want to talk about it," I say.

Mum purses her lips. "Well, just don't forget who you are."

"Okay ..." Karen says. "I think it's time for birthday activities, part B."

"There's a part B?" I stare at her.

"You, me, hot chocolate." Karen grabs my wrist. "Come on."

She plucks my birthday presents from my hands and gives them to Mum, then shoves my tote bag at me and pulls me out the door.

"Have fun," Mum calls after us.

Levi is still outside, and I concentrate on getting to

the car so I'm not tempted to look at him. I don't care what Mum said about me being rude. When I reach the car parked at the kerb I yank the door open and climb in, slamming it closed once I'm in the seat.

"Easy," Karen says from the driver's seat. "The car never did anything to you."

"Just ... drive," I say.

We pull onto the road and head towards the highway. Karen chatters non-stop on the way to the shops. I stare out the window and try not to think about how everything has become so messed up.

"Are you excited?" Karen asks.

I roll my head across the headrest and stare at her. "About what?"

Karen grips the steering wheel. "Oh my God, Katie. Schoolies!"

I smile. "Oh, that. Yeah. We'll have a blast."

"Are you kidding? It's going to rock."

"Are Jess and Stacey coming?"

Karen grins. "Of course. They have a room booked at our hotel, too."

We pull into the car park. Karen stops at the boom gate to take her ticket, then we circle the car park looking for a space. We eventually find one. My phone buzzes in my bag as I get out of the car. I glance at the screen but don't recognise the number, so I ignore it.

Karen and I walk through the busy shops and outside to the mall, passing the clock fountain on our way to the chocolate café. I remember stopping there with Levi and making a wish that we'd become something special. Seems like that's not going to come true.

Nothing

At the café I order my usual white hot chocolate, and Karen gets a dark. We sit in the back corner and sip our drinks.

"So ... how does it feel to join the eighteen club?" Karen asks.

I raise my eyebrows. "I don't feel any different."

"Come on." She sets her hot chocolate down. "You're practically a free agent now. We can go anywhere and do anything we like."

"Not quite." I laugh and take a sip of my drink. It warms my insides.

Karen smiles. "What do you want to do after this?"

"I don't know," I say. "I'm not in the greatest mood, sorry. I've been a bit of a bitch, haven't I?"

"I still love you." Karen squeezes my hand. "But seriously, you're eighteen today. We could hit the RSL."

"In the middle of the day?" I sit back in my chair.

"Don't you want your first alcoholic drink as an adult?"

"I don't want any drink, other than this delicious hot chocolate." I take another sip from my mug. "And I can have a drink at schoolies."

"Now we're talking," Karen says.

"But I'm not getting drunk. I might be eighteen today, but I'm not stupid."

"It's your birthday?" someone asks.

I look up, and Veronica is standing a few metres away from our table.

"Oh ... hey." *What is she doing here?* I force a smile. "Yeah. I'm officially an adult."

"Katie hates her birthday," Karen says. "It's the only day of the year when she's truly unhappy."

Veronica laughs, but it seems forced. "Can I sit?"

I take my tote off the seat beside me. "Um … sure. How did you know we'd be here?"

Karen stares at Veronica. I adjust my position on my chair, because the way they're looking at each other is making me uncomfortable.

Veronica slides into the seat. "Levi gave me your numbers. I tried calling you, but you didn't answer. Then I called your house. Your mum said you were here."

I'm not sure what to make of any of this. I open my mouth, but then I close it again. *Levi gave her my number?*

Karen leans on the table. "What's making you slum it today?"

Veronica leans forward to match Karen's pose. "I wanted to make sure Katie was okay."

"If this is another one of your stupid games, you can leave now."

"It's not." Veronica clenches her teeth.

"I'm fine," I say. "To be honest, I'm more worried about you. Have you reported him yet?"

Veronica rolls her eyes. "Katie, I'm okay. He didn't do anything."

"But you told him to stop, and he didn't."

Karen wrinkles her nose. "Geoff is a dick."

"You haven't told anyone, have you?" Veronica looks down at the table.

Karen sighs. "We said we wouldn't."

I let out a breath, glad that the bitchy tone has left my best friend's voice.

Veronica looks from me to Karen then back again. "For the record, I think Levi and his mates are all dicks, too."

Nothing

I press my lips together. "But you're a part of this whole dare thing."

"Yes, but after … maybe it was a bit too mean …"

Karen raises her eyebrows. "Are you trying to apologise?"

Veronica scowls. "You should hear Levi out," she says, ignoring Karen.

"What did he say to you?" I ask.

Veronica shrugs. "Just that you won't let him explain."

"That idiot asked her to the formal on a dare," Karen says. "Katie doesn't need an explanation."

Veronica gets to her feet and adjusts the strap of her purse. "There's more to the story."

"There always is," I mumble.

"Did he send you here to do his dirty work?" Karen stands, too.

"He loves you, Katie." Veronica looks down at me, and there's something in her eyes that makes me believe what she's saying.

Or maybe I just *want* to believe it.

"He has a funny way of showing it." I look away, and stare into my mug of hot chocolate.

Veronica shrugs again. "Suit yourself. See you at exams."

I stare at her back as she walks out of the café. Karen sits again and sips her drink.

"You don't believe her, do you?" she asks.

I take a deep breath. "I don't know what to believe anymore."

And I don't, because I've been burnt too often.

I'm not sure if I should give him a second chance.

5

With you

HSC exams started in the second week of term, and for the past four weeks I've been alternating between studying and taking exams. I'm confident I did well on most of them. Pretty much the only time I've left the house has been to go to school, and I've lain low enough to stay away from Levi. We only have a few subjects together anyway, so our time tables haven't crossed paths much.

I finish reading over my essay then stare at the clock on the hall wall, thinking about schoolies coming up in a couple of weeks. Jessica and Stacey are flying up, but because Karen and I are driving, we'll be leaving a day earlier and spending a night in Coffs Harbour along the way.

"Pens down," the exam supervisor says. "Please close your exam booklets and leave them on your desks. The row on my right may leave first, followed by the next, and so on."

Papers rustle, and students stand to put pens and pencil cases back in their bags. I wait until it's my row's turn, and then I file out of the hall and into the afternoon sunshine.

Jessica is waiting for me. "I have to run. Josie sent me a message. She's picking me up."

"No probs," I say. "I can train it."

She smiles and runs off towards the main entrance to the school. I make my way from the hall towards the back gate to catch the train home. Art was my last exam. Relief washes over me, and I turn my face to the sky to feel the sun's warmth.

No more exams. No more school. I can finally relax for a while.

"How do you think you went?" Veronica asks, falling into step beside me.

I shrug. "However I went."

"Have you spoken to Levi yet?"

I stop and face her. "No. What's he said now?"

"I'm getting a lift home with him. Why don't you come ask him yourself?"

I tilt my head to the side and stare at Veronica. I still can't work her out. Since the formal she's been really nice, and the last time someone was nice to me unexpectedly it turned out to be a dare. Veronica acting like this makes me uncomfortable. I'm not used to it. It's like wearing a really scratchy sweater.

"I'm not sure I'm ready to talk to him."

"Katie, it's been ages." Veronica sounds like a whiny

child. "If I have to listen to him anymore, I think I'll kill him."

"I'm okay to catch the train," I say.

"Come on." She shakes her head and grabs my arm, pulling me away from the direction of the train station and across the street.

Levi's BMW is parked up the road. Veronica shoves me at the front passenger side then gets into the back seat.

Great.

I pull the door open and get in, looking anywhere but at Levi.

"Katie," he says.

I turn to him. "Don't ..."

He takes a deep breath and starts the car, pulling away from the kerb. I wind my window down a bit and let the air blow on my face.

Levi didn't have an exam today because none of his subjects were scheduled, and I wonder what the hell he's doing here. Surely Veronica didn't ask him to pick her up. But then I think that's exactly the sort of thing Veronica would do.

"You didn't have an exam today," I say.

"Ronnie wanted a lift."

"And you're her personal chauffeur?"

Veronica snickers from the back seat. "Now you don't have to study, what're you doing tonight, Katie?"

"Sleeping," I say.

"You should come celebrate with us."

I turn in my seat so I can look into the back at her. "Let me guess: you're having a party."

"You should come." She smirks.

"Yeah, because the last time I did that it went *so* well."

"If it helps, I'll promise not to talk to you." Levi stares straight ahead.

What he should be promising is not to take any dares involving me, or not to play the stupid game in the first place.

"I think schoolies will be a good enough party for me," I say.

Levi doesn't respond. He just drives, gripping the steering wheel with one hand and resting the other on the gear stick.

"I'm not taking no for an answer," Veronica says.

I pretend I'm thinking about it. Then I actually think about it. Maybe a party would be fun. Maybe getting out of the house I've been cooped up in would be good for me.

Who am I kidding? Going to Veronica's is the worst idea ever. I'll be opening myself up for more torture and ridicule.

"If I come, can I bring Karen?" I ask, and then I regret it because there's no way I'm going to this party.

"Yes," Veronica and Levi say at the same time.

"You promised not to talk to me." I glare at Levi.

His lips curl a little, as if he's about to smile, then he stops and presses them together.

I want to look away from him, but I can't. It's been so long since I've had the opportunity to look at Levi, and I miss him. I miss his smile, and his voice, and having him climb in my window.

I miss being around him.

But I haven't only missed him for the past couple of months. I've been missing him for years.

A lump rises in my throat, and I finally turn away, staring out the side window and watching the houses go past as we turn into Veronica's street. Levi pulls over.

"I'll see you two tonight," Veronica says, getting out of the car.

We sit and watch her go inside before Levi pulls back onto the street again.

I can't look at him.

I can't let my emotions take over.

Suddenly, I feel trapped inside the car. Unable to get away from him so I don't have to face what I'm feeling. I'm stuck with nowhere to go.

My breaths come short and fast, and I squeeze my eyes closed to try and get some kind of control.

"Katie, are you okay?" Levi asks.

Am I okay?

I want to scream, *no!* But instead, I laugh. The sound is bitter. Then it starts to hurt, and a sob rises into my chest, forcing its way out of my mouth with so much force I feel like my ribs will crack. With that sob comes a cry, and my laughter turns to tears.

I put my face in my hands and cry. *Really* cry.

"Katie—?"

"No, Levi!" I yell. "I am *not* okay."

My chest rises and falls as I heave breaths in and out of my mouth. I want out of the car, but we're travelling at one hundred and ten kilometres an hour on the motorway. There's nowhere to pull over. And where would I run to anyway? I grip the door handle. We'll be home soon.

Levi moves across to the left lane and takes the next exit. It's not our exit. It's too early. At the top of the ramp

48

he turns left then right into the first side street, and pulls over, killing the engine and tugging the handbrake on.

I want out.

I need to get out of the car.

My fingers grapple with the handle, and I cry harder because I can't get it to work. Then the door opens and I spill onto the grass. I stumble to my feet and run, but I don't get far before I trip and collapse on the ground—a blubbery, snotty mess. I draw my knees to my chest and put my head on them, sucking in deep breaths.

Levi sits beside me. He doesn't say anything. He just sits there. I concentrate on slowing my breathing, because what else can I do? I can't get up and walk home, and it's obvious Levi isn't going anywhere.

"Katie," he finally says.

I squeeze my eyes closed. "What?"

"Let's get you home."

I nod, and he helps me to my feet. I should be embarrassed at having a complete breakdown in front of the one person I've loved my entire life. The person who caused the breakdown to begin with. But I'm not embarrassed. I've known Levi for so long, and I'm glad he's had the chance to finally see what his actions have done to me.

He reaches out and puts his arms around me. Instead of fighting him, I fall into his embrace and press my face into his neck. It brings back the memory of how we were dancing before our first real kiss. That memory makes my heart smile when smiling is the last thing I feel like doing.

"I want to explain everything to you," Levi says.

I pull away. "I'm not sure an explanation will make

any difference."

Levi rubs my back in circles, and for a moment I let him, then I step away. I'm not going to allow him to do this now. Not while I'm weak and emotional, and not thinking straight. I take another step back, and he drops his hand to his side.

"Let's go home." He walks to the car and I follow.

We don't speak for the rest of the drive. I turn the radio on to drown out my thoughts, but it's not that effective. I wish I could go home and not have Levi there, right next door, in my face all the time. Maybe if we had some distance everything would work out in its own time. Right now, I feel smothered, with nowhere to run.

Levi pulls into his driveway, and I get out of the car as soon as he kills the engine. I shoulder my bag, and cross over to my yard.

"Will I see you tonight?" Levi asks.

I turn and face him. "Maybe."

He nods and I go inside. No one is home yet. I'm grateful, because I can go straight to my room and get rid of any of the breakdown episode evidence. I dump my stuff and go to the bathroom, washing my face and taking my contacts out.

I stare at my reflection and push my glasses onto my nose. There was a time when they were a big part of me. Now, they're only a side thought. Nothing important. Like I was a side thought to Levi. Not important enough for him to consider my feelings instead of his reputation.

Another tear slips down my cheek and I swipe at it, turning away from the mirror.

I'm not going to this party.

Nothing

All I want to do is curl up in bed with my headphones in and write in my journal.

Back in my room my phone rings. I fumble around in the bottom of my tote bag, pulling it out. Karen's name flashes on the screen and I swipe it to answer.

"Hey." I flop onto my bed.

"How'd you go?"

"Fine. It was fine. Can we not talk about exams ever again?"

Karen laughs. "Done. Did you talk to Jess?"

"She had to go meet her mum after, so not really. Why?"

Karen pauses and I listen to her breathing.

"There's a party tonight," she finally says.

I roll onto my side and put my phone between my ear and my pillow, then grab my bunny and play with its ears.

"I know."

"At Veronica's," Karen says.

"Yep."

"We should go."

I sigh. "You should go. I should stay home."

"Come on, Katie. Jess is going. We'll have safety in numbers. Everything is different now. School is over. Exams are finished. We need to celebrate. And those bitches don't rule us anymore. This is our chance to show them that nothing from the past matters from today onwards." Karen goes quiet again.

I take my glasses off, close my eyes, and hug my bunny to my chest. Nothing from the past matters? Everything from my past matters. It's shaped me to be the person I am, and my past is what has put me in the position I'm in. "If it weren't for my past, I wouldn't be—"

"Stop it," Karen says. "This is exactly what I mean. *Nothing* matters. We have our future in front of us. Screw them. And screw Levi for what he's done. Tonight you can either stay home and choose to let them beat you, or you can walk in there and party like you've never partied before."

"I'm not sure I want to face him after what happened this afternoon," I say.

"Oh my God, what now?" Karen asks.

I take a deep breath. "I may have had a breakdown in front of him." I pause. "He drove me home and on the way I ... cried a lot."

"Oh, Katie. Are you okay?"

I laugh, so hard it brings tears to my eyes. And I can hear the frown in Karen's voice when she says, "What's so funny?"

My laughter subsides. I get control of myself and wipe my eyes. "That's exactly what Levi asked me, and it set me off."

"Well, at least he knows how much of a jerk he's been. Hopefully you dug his cold heart out of his chest and warmed it up a bit."

"I still don't want to face him."

"You can, and you will," Karen says.

"You're not going to take no for an answer, are you?" I ask.

"I've already told Jess to pick us up at eight. I'll be there in half an hour, and we can plot your revenge."

I laugh. "I don't want revenge ... I want Levi."

"Stop talking nonsense. See you in a bit."

Nothing

Karen hangs up, and I roll onto my back, staring at my phone. It rings again while I'm holding it, and this time 'Mum' flashes on the screen.

"Hey, Mum."

"Katie, honey. How was your last exam?"

"Fine. Like all the others."

"How are you feeling?" Mum asks.

I stop myself before I say 'fine' again. "I'm good. Got home not long ago."

"Great. Can you fix yourself something tonight?" Mum asks. "Your Dad is taking me to a movie."

"Sure. What about Daniel?"

"He's a big boy. He'll probably be out."

"Actually, I'll be out as well," I say. "Veronica's having another party. You know, to celebrate our transition into the real world."

Mum chuckles. "Okay. You know your curfew. I'll see you in the morning."

"Bye, Mum." I end the call and toss my phone on the bed.

I close my eyes, and try to clear my head of everything, but thinking about nothing is pretty much impossible. No matter how hard I try, my thoughts keep going back to Levi. What if he does have a good explanation for what he did? What if all I need to do is listen? But then what if I do, and we work at building our relationship again, but then it all gets stripped away like it has before? Do I really want to take that chance?

Can I put myself out there again?

Hot tears sting my eyes, and I shove the heels of my hands into them.

No. It's better to keep my distance and not get involved with him again. With anyone.

I'll go to this party, but I'll stay away from Levi.

The doorbell rings, and I wipe my eyes then get up to go downstairs. When I open the door, Karen is standing on the step with a big smile on her face, and a backpack slung over her shoulder.

"Why so happy?" I ask.

Karen pushes past me and into the foyer. "We have work to do."

"What are you talking about?" I close the front door.

"Makeover." She walks up the stairs. At the top, she looks down at me. "We can do our nails and hair. You're going to rock this party, and we're going to make Levi rue the day he *ever* decided to fuck with you."

6

Good one

*K*aren sits on my bed and pulls all sorts of items from her backpack, spreading them over my quilt.

"Go and put your contacts in," she says.

"But I only took them out when I got home."

"I don't care." She stares at me. "You're not wearing your glasses to this party."

Reluctantly, I go to the bathroom and put my lenses in. Back in my room I sit in my desk chair. Karen sweeps a makeup wipe over my face, followed by a loaded powder brush.

"Close your eyes," she says.

I do as she asks. "I want to look natural. Not like a hooker."

"Stop worrying. You will not look cheap."

I sit for another ten minutes as Karen works on my

face, but I've pretty much had enough. Two minutes of this is too long. "Are you finished?"

"Gloss your lips," she says. "Then you're done."

I jump up and rummage around in my tote bag to find my favourite lip gloss, then stand in front of the full-length mirror on my wardrobe door. A smile spreads across my face when I look at my reflection. I definitely don't look like a hooker, and Karen has done an amazing job of making my skin glow. She's put the slightest hint of pink into my cheeks, filled out my lashes, and added sparkle to the lids of my eyes. I swipe my gloss over my lips to complete the soft look.

"Now ... clothes," Karen says. "You have to look hot."

"Jeans and a top will be fine." I open my wardrobe and pull out my favourite pair of jeans.

Karen digs into her bag again. "Nope. Put those away. You're wearing these."

She holds up a pair of dark skinny jeans—the kind I would never be able to afford. They have a really fine silver sparkle in the fabric. She hands them to me and I take them, feeling the thickness of the good-quality denim. So much nicer than my old thin pair.

"I can't wear these," I say. "Everyone will know I can't afford them."

"Don't be an idiot. I just gave them to you, so they're yours. You can say they were a birthday present if anyone asks."

I bite my lip, and look down at the jeans in my hands. They're so nice, and I've never owned a pair from anywhere other than a cheap department store.

"Thank you." I hug Karen, and she pats my back.

Nothing

We both shimmy into our jeans. Karen's are light blue and have fashionable rips in the legs, and they hug her in all the right places. She looks amazing. I sift through my wardrobe, searching for a top to wear, but I don't have anything good enough to complement the jeans. Karen tries to give me her black top that also has sparkles embedded into the slinky fabric, but I don't let her.

"I want to go simple," I say. "You know I'm not a fancy kinda girl."

I pull out a plain white singlet top, one with wide straps, and put it on over my nicest bra.

"Good choice," Karen says. "It shows off your boobs."

"Stop looking at my boobs." I grab my favourite black ankle boots from the bottom of the wardrobe, and sit on the edge of the bed to put them on.

Karen shrugs. "You have nice boobs."

She grins, and puts on a tight black sleeveless top that zips up at the front. Then she slips her feet into a cute pair of strappy black heels. Karen sits beside me on the bed, digs into her bag, and pulls out a few bottles of nail polish. She chooses a shimmery aqua and gives it a shake before setting to work on her toenails.

"No point me doing mine." I look down at my shoes.

"Do your nails." Karen glances at the clock above my desk. "We're not meeting Jess out the front for another twenty minutes."

I search through the bottles lying on the bed between us and go for a bright purple. I coat my fingernails as carefully as I can, blowing on them to get them to dry faster. Karen coats her fingernails as well, then we head downstairs. I opt not to take my purse or a bag this time, so I slip my driver's licence into my phone cover along with a twenty. We lock the front door with the hidden spare key, and walk to the road to wait for Jessica.

"Josie is driving," Karen says. "Jess said she'd drive us home."

"Like Josie would give her any other choice." I tuck my hair behind my ear and check my phone.

A crash comes from Levi's house, like a plate smashing or something hitting the tiled floor inside. Someone yells. Then more yelling. I recognise Levi's voice but I can't make out his words.

"What's going on?" Karen looks towards Levi's place.

The front door flies open, banging onto the outside wall of the house. Levi tumbles onto the veranda, but it's not until his dad is standing in the doorway that I realise Levi didn't fall. Mark pushed him.

Yvonne clings to Mark's arm, trying to pull him back inside. Levi gets to his feet and his gaze meets mine before he quickly looks away. I'm aware that my mouth is open, but I don't close it. I stand frozen with my phone in my hands, gaping at my neighbours who are obviously arguing about something. Only Levi's dad hasn't seen us yet.

Mark steps towards Levi. "You will show some respect—"

"Or what, Dad?" Levi yells. "You'll make me? I'm not scared of you."

"You should be."

I step forward. "Levi, is everything okay?"

Mark turns in my direction, his eyes widening. Then his brow narrows into a frown. He says something to Levi that I can't hear before going inside with Yvonne and slamming the door behind them.

"I'm not Mason," Levi screams. He stands on the veranda, staring at the door, his shoulders heaving, his fists clenched at his sides.

A car sounds behind us, and I glance over my shoulder as Josephine pulls up to the kerb. She winds her window down. "Get in, bitches."

"Charming." Karen opens the back passenger door.

I glance at Levi. He's sitting on the steps of his veranda with his head in his hands.

"Hang on." I walk towards Levi.

"Katie, what are you doing?" Karen asks.

I wave her away and keep walking until I reach the veranda. Asking him if he's okay is a stupid thing to do because he obviously isn't. And I hate it when people ask me that question.

"Are you coming to the party?" I ask instead.

Levi raises his head, then sits up straighter. "You look really nice, Katie."

I shift on my feet and fidget with my phone. "Thanks."

"I have no car," Levi says. "Dad took my keys."

"Come on, Katie," Josephine yells.

I glance back at her, then look at Levi. "Come with us."

Levi gets to his feet. "That would involve you and me being in the car together."

"I've gotten pretty good at ignoring you." I offer him a small smile.

Levi drops his gaze to the ground. I grab his hand and pull so he'll follow.

Heat.

Warmth.

Levi.

It hits me all at once.

I let go of his hand before I want to hold it forever. It feels too good.

Levi stands at Josephine's window. "Room for me?"

She nods. "Get in."

Levi opens the passenger side back door and I climb in, scooting across to the middle so I'm sandwiched between Levi and Karen.

It's impossible to talk on the drive to Veronica's because Josephine cranks the music and winds her window down. I don't mind. It's not like I have much to say to Levi anyway.

Every now and then I catch Karen glaring at him, but he's not looking at her. Whenever I chance a look at him he's staring at me, and I press my knees together to try and make myself as small as possible in the middle of the back seat.

Levi's leg and shoulder rest against mine, making me warm, and I sit rigid because I don't want to relax and make him think I'm comfortable. I concentrate on staring ahead through the front windscreen, and I let my hair fall over my face like a curtain.

We pull into Veronica's street, and something touches my hair. I flinch and realise it's Levi, holding his hand out. It hovers in front of my face, then he tucks my hair behind my ear.

Josephine parks on the street and turns the car off, the music dying with it. I stare at Levi who still has his hand in my hair. He smiles, his lips curling slightly, and

Nothing

I get lost in his eyes. The way he's looking at me turns my stomach to mush, and I want to throw myself at him and slap him at the same time.

I'm not prepared for the way he's making me feel, sitting so close to him in such a confined space. I'm supposed to be angry with him. After what he did, I never wanted to see him again, and yet here we are.

Slowly, I reach up and wrap my fingers around his wrist then pull so his hand comes away from my face.

"Please, don't," I say.

We're close enough that I could lean forward and kiss him. My heart wants to, but my head stops me. I want him, but I don't, all at the same time. How can I want someone so badly who has hurt me the way Levi has?

One of the car doors slams, and then another.

"Come on, lovebirds," Josephine says from the footpath. Through the window, I see her standing with Jessica.

"Katie?" Karen is still in the seat beside me.

"I'm good," I say. "I'll get out Levi's side."

Karen's door closes a few seconds later and I'm alone in the car with Levi, my hand still gripping his wrist.

"I'm not going to give up on you," he says.

I let go of him. "Can we get out now, please?"

He shakes his head. "I love you."

"What?" I breathe.

But he doesn't answer. Levi throws his door open and gets out. I stare at his back as he walks towards Veronica's front door. There's no one out on the porch tonight like there was at the last party. Levi doesn't turn around, and it's not until Karen bends down and fills my line of sight that I move to get out of the car.

"What did he say to you?" she asks.

"Nothing." I'm not going to tell anyone what he said, because repeating it won't make it true.

Josephine locks the car, and we follow Levi's path to the house. Inside, Rachel, Jarred, and Geoff are in the lounge room, along with a few others from school. The sight of Geoff makes me sick, and I cringe when he looks at me. I can't believe Veronica has let him in her house after what he did to her. The coffee table has several bottles of booze on it, and a few bottles of water.

Veronica comes out of the kitchen with plastic cups, a bottle of Coke, and a bottle of orange juice, followed by Levi who has three cans of beer in his hands. Our eyes meet, and I want to ask him not to drink, but I'm not the boss of him. I make a note to talk to him later and find out what's really going on with his dad.

He sets two of the cans on the coffee table.

Veronica pours herself a bourbon and Coke. "You made it." She smiles, and I'm surprised at how genuine she seems.

"Hey." I smile back.

"Pick your poison." She points to the table, taking a sip from her cup.

"Don't mind if I do." Karen fixes herself a vodka and orange.

"I'll have a beer." I grab one of the cans. I figure beer is less lethal.

Jessica takes a bottle of water.

Josephine joins Rachel on one of the big lounges. I set my phone on the coffee table and sit on the lounge opposite them with Karen and Jessica. Jarred makes a big display of going over to Josephine and kissing her in front of everyone. My eyes widen and I look to Jessica, who shrugs.

"What did I miss?" I ask.

"Apparently a lot," Karen says, settling back into her seat. "But so did I."

Veronica comes over and drops onto the arm of the lounge beside me. "Jarred and I haven't been together since the formal. I much prefer being single." She glares at him, then she glares at Geoff.

Levi takes a seat in an armchair near the open fireplace and sips his beer.

"Where is everyone?" I look at the cold can in my hand. I haven't taken a sip yet.

"Small party tonight." Veronica looks down at me. "Mum and Dad got a bit funny after the last one."

Josephine gets up so Jarred can sit down. "Who's going first?" Jarred says as he pulls her onto his lap.

I raise my eyebrows. "First for what?"

"Come on, Katie," Rachel says. "You should be a pro at truth or dare by now."

I grit my teeth and frown. "What makes you think I want to play?"

"Come on guys," Veronica says. "Do we have to?"

"We always do," Geoff says.

"Doesn't mean we should now." I look at each person in the room.

Veronica sighs. "Okay. No one has to do anything they don't want to. Only solid rule is you can't truth or dare the person who just truth or dared you. I thought maybe we could have some harmless fun this time."

"Harmless?" I stand. "You think this game is harmless?"

Levi looks up at me from his seat, and takes another sip of his beer.

"This game is stupid," Karen says.

"No, hang on." I sit again and take a big gulp from my can. "You want to play, I'll play. Let's have some *fun*." I stare at Levi. "Truth or dare?"

He sits forward and puts his beer on the coffee table. "Truth."

"Why did you accept the dare to ask me to the formal?" Looks like I do want to know the truth, as much as I've tried to deny it.

Levi's stare bores into mine. "Because I wanted to take you."

"You couldn't have asked me anyway?"

"That's two questions," Rachel says. "You only get one. Levi's turn."

Everyone waits.

Levi picks up his beer and takes a deep drink. "Josie, truth or dare?"

"Truth," she says.

Levi sits back. "Have you and Jess ever twin-swapped where it involved you being with your sister's boyfriend?" He raises his eyebrows, and a chuckle makes its way around the room.

Josephine hesitates and glances at Jessica. "Yes."

"Oh my God, who?" Karen sits forward.

"I don't have to answer that," Josephine says. "My turn ... Karen, truth or dare?"

"Dare," she says. "Might as well make this interesting."

Josephine sits forward on Jarred's knees and grins.

"Choose one boy in the room then stand with your back to the rest of us and flash him."

Karen jumps up. "Okay, Jarred, let's go. Behind the lounge." She walks around our seat and leans against the back of it.

Josephine's smile drops away. Jarred moves Josephine off his lap so he can follow Karen, and Geoff and the others whoop and catcall. Josephine crosses her arms over her chest and stands with her hip cocked. Her frown is so deep she has shadows from the lines between her eyes.

"You asked for it," Levi says, popping another can of beer.

"You ready?" Karen asks.

Jarred's eyes go wide as Karen lifts her top. More hollers fill the room. Then Geoff reaches out and grabs Karen's boob as she's pulling her top down. She spins around and lashes out, catching the edge of Geoff's jaw with her fingertips.

"Ouch!" Geoff cries.

"Really?" I jump to my feet and shove him. He falls onto the screen around the fireplace. "You deserve more than that."

"I was just having *fun*," he says.

Levi gets up and grabs Geoff by the collar, pushing him towards the other lounge. "Go and sit down, you idiot."

I look at Karen as she finishes adjusting her top, and mouth *you okay?*

She nods, and comes to sit back down, taking up Veronica's old position on the arm of the lounge with her feet on the seat cushion. Veronica is quiet and stares at her hands, and I get the feeling she's remembering what Geoff did to her at the formal. Why anyone is friends with him is beyond me.

"Geoff," Karen says. "Truth or dare?"

"Dare." He smiles. "You're not getting anything from me."

Karen bites her lip. If I were her, I'd be thinking of making him do something that would embarrass the shit out of him. Maybe bring him down a few pegs and put him in his place. But then again, not much fazes guys like Geoff.

"I dare you to kiss Jarred … on the mouth. Open. With tongue," she says.

Geoff sniggers and sits back. "No way. We don't have to do anything we don't want to. Ronnie's rules."

"What, you scared?" I ask. "It's just a kiss."

"I don't do guys." He looks at Veronica and licks his lips. I cringe. He is such a sleaze.

"Then you forfeit your turn," Karen says. "Pick someone to go next."

"Rachel. You can go." Geoff takes a big swallow of his bourbon.

"Katie, truth or dare," she says.

I should have known she'd pick me. Everyone stares at me, waiting for my answer.

"Dare," I say.

Jarred raises his eyebrows. "Wow, I wasn't expecting that."

"Make it good," Geoff says.

Rachel claps her hands and squeals. "Oh, this is fun. Ten minutes in the closet with one guy in this room. No lights."

I raise my eyebrows. "That's it?"

I'm trying to act cool when really I'm freaking out.

"Pick Levi," Karen whispers in my ear. "But if he touches you I'll kill him."

I turn my nose up. There is not one boy in this room who I want to spend ten minutes in the dark with right now, Levi included. I'm not sure I'm ready to be alone with him.

"Come on, say it." Rachel smirks. "We know who you want."

"Katie, you don't have to," Karen says.

"You didn't have to flash anyone either," I say.

She smiles, and I love her because she knows that just like her, I'm not going to back down from a dare.

I get up from my seat and walk to the door set into the side of the huge staircase that leads to the upper floor. I stop and face everyone, shoving my fingertips into the front pockets of my jeans.

"Levi," I say, and the room erupts with whistles and whoops. I'm surrounded by a bunch of immature, hormonal idiots.

I don't miss the smile on Levi's face before he looks at his feet and stands. He sets his beer on the coffee table and walks slowly towards me. He probably thinks we're going to make out, but that's the last thing I want to do with him right now. No, I'm going to tell him that I'm finally ready to listen to him and hear what he has to say.

His excuse for what he did to me better be a good one.

Forgive yourself

When Levi reaches me, he takes one of my hands and gives it a squeeze.

"You don't have to do this," he says.

"I know." I smile with my lips closed.

I open the door, and pull him into the closet. The door clicks closed behind us, and I freeze in the darkness. I feel disoriented because I can't see anything. The only thing anchoring me is the fact I'm still holding Levi's hand.

There's a murmur of voices outside, and someone wolf whistles again. If the lights were on I'm sure Levi would notice the blush creeping up my neck. The heat prickles my skin. I wasn't embarrassed out there, but now we're alone, it's different.

"I don't want to make out with you," I say.

"I know." Levi's breath is hot on my ear, and it startles

me. He's breathing in short breaths, and my heart races.

"We have ten minutes," I say.

"Probably nine now." I hear a smile in his voice.

"This isn't funny," I say around a smile. "I want the truth."

I stand in the dark and wait. Heaviness surrounds me as Levi lets go of my hand. For a second, I panic, not knowing what's in front of me or behind me.

"What's wrong?" Levi asks. "Your breathing's changed."

"I ... It's dark." I clasp my hands together and stand still.

His hands find my waist and he pulls me close. His warm breath is beside my ear again.

"The truth?" he asks.

"All of it." I swallow. "Why did you ask me to the formal?"

"Because I wanted to." His grip tightens on my waist. "And before you say anything, that *is* the truth. And if I didn't ask you, then Geoff would have. Veronica dared him to first."

I scoff. "That bitch! But there's no way I would have said yes to him." I shudder, and Levi laughs.

"I was trying to protect you, Katie."

"Seriously, that's it? That's your excuse?" I ask. "I'm a big girl, Levi. I can look after myself."

"You don't know Geoff like I do."

"I have a pretty good idea of what he's like. But I'm guessing he didn't tell you about the toilet brush incident."

"The what?"

"I promised Veronica I wouldn't say anything."

"You can trust me, Katie."

Now it's my turn to laugh. "Can I?"

"We all know Geoff has trouble keeping his hands to himself."

"Yeah, well. Veronica found out the hard way." I pause. "He was getting a bit hot and heavy with her in the girls' bathroom at the formal. She said no. He didn't listen. I whacked him with a toilet brush."

"He said he and Ronnie got it on, which is why Jarred broke up with her, but Geoff did *not* tell me that. I should've guessed."

"I told Veronica to report him, but she wouldn't."

Levi adjusts his hold on me. His fingers splay across my lower back. "Can you see now that I was trying to protect you from him?"

"That doesn't explain the money—"

"Geoff accepted the dare to ask you to the formal, but Jarred wanted to make it a bit more interesting. He dared Geoff to sleep with you as well."

"They're both jerks," I say.

"Yeah. That's when I said I'd give them a hundred bucks each to leave you alone. But they only agreed after I said I'd take on the dares myself."

"So you *were* dared to take me to the formal?"

"Only because I wanted to. I wasn't going to let Geoff near you."

I chew my lip. "And did you pay them?"

Levi's breath tickles my cheek. "Yes, but not once did I ever consider forcing you to sleep with me. I would never have done that. Can you forgive me for all of this?"

I take a deep breath, and let it out slowly. "That depends."

"On what?"

70

"You can't say all this and expect me to be okay with any of it. I have big trust issues with you now."

Levi pulls me close again and presses his hands firmly into the small of my back. It's so dark I'm scared what will happen if I try to pull away. I'll probably end up tripping over something, and falling on the floor. But I'm scared what will happen if I don't pull away either.

I stiffen, holding my arms between us and clasping my hands together. I'm not sure where else to put them. Levi presses his forehead to mine.

"How can I get you to trust me again?" His breath tickles my lips.

"Trust is earned, Levi. I—"

He crushes his lips to mine, and I press my hands to his chest.

I didn't want him to kiss me.

I'm not ready for this ... am I?

Light pours over us, and Levi pulls away.

I blink at the glare.

"Time's up," Veronica says. "Looks like you two have been having fun."

I stare at Levi, and run for the front door.

"Katie," Levi yells. "Katie, stop."

Levi's kisses are amazing, but this was a mistake. I can't trust him. I can't trust anyone. I reach the street and look around. The street lamps cast pools of light on the footpath. I spot Josephine's car. She drove us here. How am I going to get home?

I turn in the direction of the train station, déjà vu washing over me. I've been here before, and Levi was the one making me run last time as well. Why do I keep letting this happen? What is it about him that I can't stay away from? Every time I go back, every time I think we might have something worth fighting for, he reduces it to nothing again.

He keeps hurting me over and over.

"Leave her alone," Karen yells, and I stop to look back at Veronica's house. Karen grabs Levi's arm so he faces her. She shoves him in the chest, and he takes a step back. "You have been a dick to her too many times. I'm not going to let you hurt her again."

Levi steps towards Karen. "You don't even know what happened in there."

"She's running, so I can take a pretty good guess." Karen's voice is loud, and I glance around to see if anyone else has come out of the house.

I twist my fingers together. *What do I do?* Getting out of here and away from Levi is my number-one priority, but then I look at my hands and remember that I left my phone on the coffee table in the house.

I have to go back.

"When are you going to realise she would do anything for you?" Karen says, her voice sounding louder again as I walk towards them.

"I would do anything for her." Levi is yelling as well.

"You have a funny way of showing it." Karen folds her arms over her chest.

"Can you guys stop, please?" I say when I reach them.

Karen and Levi look at me. Levi runs a hand through his hair, and I close my eyes for a second, hating the effect he has on me.

Karen comes to my side. "You okay?"

Nothing

"I really wish people would stop asking me that," I say. "I'm going to get my phone."

Inside, the others are sitting around the coffee table, laughing about God knows what. Me, probably. But I'm beyond caring. I'm tired, and I want to go home.

Jessica stands up. "Katie, are you—"

"I'm. Fine." I grab my phone from the coffee table. "Any chance we could go?"

Jessica looks from me to Josephine.

"Go." Josephine waves a hand at her sister. "Jarred can bring me home later."

I don't wait for another response from Jessica, heading to the front door and back outside into the warm summer night air. Karen and Levi are down on the footpath at the end of the driveway. Their discussion looks heated, but at least they've stopped yelling.

I walk past both of them to Josephine's car. The hazard lights flash and the locks pop. Jessica must have pushed the button on the keyring. I grab the front passenger door handle and rip the door open, ready to be done with tonight. After I slide into the seat I take a deep breath to calm myself, and rest my head against the headrest.

For a moment, I wonder why I'm so angry. Levi kissed me when I'd told him I didn't want that, but I still liked it. Am I overreacting? He didn't keep going like Geoff did with Veronica. Levi backed off as soon as I pushed him away, so am I angry that he kissed me, or am I angry because being angry with him is easier than letting him in?

I cover my face with my hands and close my eyes. There are voices outside the car but they're muffled, and

I don't try to make out the words they're saying. A moment later, Jessica climbs into the driver's seat, and Karen gets in the back.

There's a tap on my window. I wait for Jessica to start the car before taking my hands away from my face. Levi is at the window making a circular motion with his hand for me to wind the window down. I press the button on the door and let it down halfway.

"Can I get a lift home, too?" he asks.

I shrug and look out the front windscreen. "Not my car."

Jessica sighs. "What are we going to do with you two? Just ... get in."

"Great," Karen says.

Levi goes around to the driver's side and gets in the back. I close my eyes again, and wait for Jessica to start driving. I keep my eyes closed for most of the trip.

No one speaks.

When we reach Karen's place, she squeezes my shoulder, and whispers in my ear, "Call you tomorrow."

I nod but I don't reply. I like the quiet right now.

Jessica continues on to our street, dropping Levi and I outside our houses. She offers me a small smile. I thank her for the lift, then get out of the car and watch her until she turns into her driveway up the road.

I don't look at Levi or talk to him as I make my way to my front door. I feel his presence behind me though, and when I reach my steps I turn around to face him.

He stands with his hands stuffed into his pockets. "I'm sorry. I shouldn't have kissed you when you said you didn't want me to."

Nothing

I press my lips together. "No. You shouldn't have."

We stand and look at each other for what feels like forever. There are so many thoughts running through my head, and so many feelings pounding at my heart. I don't know which way is up, down, left, or right. I feel as if I've been torn apart and then put back together again a million times over, and it hurts.

I wish I could explain all of this to him so he'd understand.

"You can't kiss me and think everything will be okay." I clutch my phone with both hands. "And you can't kiss me after I've told you not to."

Levi runs a hand down his face, and rubs the back of his neck. "How else do I apologise? I've already said I'm sorry, and tried to explain what I did."

"That was an apology?" I ask. "You kissed me to apologise?"

"No ... yes. No. I kissed you because I wanted to." Levi shakes his head and stares at his feet before looking up again and locking his gaze on mine. "Can we start again?"

I close my eyes and take a breath. "Ask me in the morning," I say, opening my eyes again. "Everything always looks better in the morning."

Levi smiles and nods. "Okay."

"Okay."

"Good night, Katie."

I wait until he's back on his side of the lawn before I unlock the door as quietly as I can, and go up to my room. I'm pretty sure no one is home because our driveway is empty. I hope Mum and Dad are having a good time.

When I get to my room I toss my phone on the bed, and pull my PJs from under my pillow. I change quickly, then go to my window seat and pick up my journal. I sit and tuck my legs beneath me.

Tonight totally sucked. I should never have gone to that party. I think I said that last time, so I obviously didn't learn my lesson.

Veronica was being okay for once. She wanted to play nicely. But Levi ... what am I going to do? I don't know anything anymore.

I don't know what to think about everything he told me. Can I really believe he asked me to the formal to protect me?

He ripped my heart out and stomped on it, but every time I look at him, he melts me.

Is it possible to love someone and hate them all at the same time?

I stop writing, and bite the end of my pen. Out of habit, I glance over to Levi's place. He's sitting on the bottom step leading up to his veranda, his face in his hands. There's something at his feet, and it's not until he picks it up that I realise it's a bourbon bottle.

He's drinking again.

Where did he get it from? I didn't notice him having anything when he got in the car, but then again, I didn't look at him during the ride home.

Why is he doing this to himself?

The front door to Levi's house opens, and his dad steps out. Levi looks over his shoulder then gets to his feet, the bottle in one hand. I don't have to hear what Mark says to know he's angry. It's written all over his face. He clenches his fists, and takes a step towards Levi.

I kneel up on my window seat, and push the bottom part of the window open, then press my palms to the windowsill. I shouldn't be watching or listening, but I want to know what's going on. Obviously, Levi's dad isn't happy about Levi's drinking. I guess if my other son had died because of alcohol, I wouldn't like it either.

Levi's dad rushes at him and rips the bottle from his hand, pouring the contents onto the front lawn. Levi tries to grab for the bottle but Mark shoves him away. Levi falls hard onto the path, his hands flying out to break his fall. He gets to a sitting position and stares at his palms. I can't see if they're bloody, but I'm guessing they are.

"This has to stop," Mark yells, standing over Levi.

Levi's shoulders shake as if he's crying. "Why?" he yells. "You don't understand."

"No, *you* don't understand. You'll end up where your brother is." Mark goes back up the steps and inside, slamming the front door.

"Maybe that's where I belong," Levi yells after him, then he falls onto the path and covers his face with his hands.

My heart breaks a little bit more.

Levi rolls onto his side, and I catch his gaze as he looks up to my window. Now I regret pulling the lattice off the side of the house, because if it was still there I would ask him to climb it.

I've been so selfish, focusing on myself when Levi has been hurting like this after the death of his brother. Maybe Levi is more broken than I realised.

I jump off the window seat and go to my door, stopping

on the threshold to the hallway. Do I want to go out there? I'm the only one around to help. But can I do that, or will I make it worse? Can I put aside my hurt and anger to help him with his?

What have I got to lose? He needs someone.

I take the stairs two at a time and burst out the front door. By the time I make it onto my front lawn, Levi is sitting with his knees bent and his arms resting on them. I stop at our boundary and take a deep breath.

"What do you want, Katie?" he asks.

"To help ... if I can."

Levi shakes his head. "No one can help me. I'm too messed up."

"That's not true." I walk over and sit on the grass near him.

"Yeah it is. I screwed everything up with us, and I'm just ... following in my brother's footsteps."

"You are *not* Mason." I play with the grass in front of me, tugging at the spiky leaves and breaking some off.

"What I am is a disappointment."

"That's not true either," I say. "You were our school captain. You had so many people looking up to you, and being proud of you."

Levi scoffs. "Yeah, because of who my parents are, and how much money we have. I've been nothing but an embarrassment. Not like you." He moves to the grass and lies down. "You got to where you are because you worked for it."

"And you think that's been easy?" I lie beside him and look up at the stars.

"Would you rather have had it handed to you?" Levi

rolls his head to the side, but I don't move to look at him.

"No. I don't want anything handed to me. If I can't achieve something myself then it's not worth it."

"Exactly." Levi sighs. "Mason was a hard worker. He got everything he wanted because he earned it. Then because of me he made one mistake, and he lost his life. *I* lost him. He was my motivation, my support, my everything. Without him, I'm nothing."

This time, I roll my head to the side to look at Levi. He keeps staring at the night sky. He blinks, and a tear rolls from the corner of his eye.

I slip my hand into his. "I know how you feel, but you need to stop blaming yourself."

"How could you possibly know?" This time he does look at me. His eyes glisten in the moonlight.

"You may not be dead," I say. "But I lost you for a long time."

Levi squeezes his eyes closed, and more tears find their way onto his cheeks.

I roll onto my side, and put my other hand on his chest over his heart. It beats softly under my fingertips. "Mason's accident wasn't your fault."

"I gave him back his keys," Levi says. "I promised Dad I wouldn't, but I did it anyway, because I could never say no to Mason."

"Mason made the choice to drive that night, not you," I say. "You are *not* responsible for someone else's actions. Only for your own."

"And I've made some amazing choices, haven't I?"

I give his hand another squeeze. Levi may not have made the best decisions about a lot of things, but I probably haven't either.

I smile. "We're here now. We're alive, and the past is in the past. We all make mistakes, Levi; we can't change them. And maybe it's not just me who has to forgive you for the things you've done. Maybe you need to find a way to forgive yourself."

Start living again

*I*t's been two weeks since I laid on the front lawn with Levi, staring at the stars. We haven't spoken much since then, and I think he's keeping his distance to give me some space, but now I'm leaving with Karen to head north for schoolies, and I wish Levi and I had made the time to resolve things a bit more.

Karen pulls into my driveway, and I roll my suitcase to the car.

"Don't do anything stupid," Daniel says, following me.

I smirk. "Me? As if."

Daniel shrugs. "Dad told me to say that."

"He couldn't say it himself?" I glance over my shoulder as Mum and Dad come through the front door.

Karen jumps out of the car and pops the boot. Daniel lifts my case in and wedges it beside Karen's. I swear she's packed for a month away, not nine nights.

"Seriously, Katie." Daniel slams the boot closed. "Have fun, but look after each other."

Karen punches Daniel on the arm. "You can cut the 'concerned big brother' act now."

"Bring my sister back in one piece." Daniel punches her back, but not as hard.

"She's in the best hands." Karen winks, and grins at my brother.

Mum and Dad come over, and they both hold me tight. You'd think I was going away for a year.

"Make sure you call us when you reach Coffs Harbour," Mum says.

"And drive safely." Dad looks from Karen to me, and back again.

"Don't worry, Bill. We'll be extra careful." Karen beams at my parents.

Mum and Dad go back to the veranda, and Daniel hugs me before following them.

"Spend that money wisely," he calls over his shoulder.

I laugh then look at Karen. We both squeal, and I run around to the passenger side of the car. As I open it, I hear the screen door squeak over at Levi's house. I lean on the top of the car door and watch him walk down his front steps. Karen starts the car and Levi quickens his pace.

"Will I see you up at Surfers?" Levi asks when he reaches me.

I smile. "I guess. Maybe ... hopefully." My cheeks burn, and I bite my lip.

He shoves his hands into his pockets and rocks on his heels. "We're bound to run into each other somewhere."

Nothing

"Probably," I say. "But, you know … you can go and have fun with your mates. Don't worry about me."

"I always worry about you." Levi stares at me, and I wish we didn't have the car door between us, because I want to hug him.

"Maybe a holiday is what we both need. Time away from home might help us figure everything out," I say, even though I know all I want is Levi. All I've ever wanted is him; he's just made it really hard.

I move to get in the car.

"Katie?" Levi says.

I straighten again. "Yes?"

He reaches out and tucks a lock of my hair behind my ear. "Look after yourself." Then he leans in and gives me a kiss on the forehead.

I smile and nod, then drop into the passenger seat of Karen's mum's car. Levi gently closes the door, and when I go to press the button to wind the window all the way down, Karen is already doing it.

Levi leans on the window opening, and bends down to look in. "Can I call you?"

"Sure," I say. "That would be nice."

"Have a safe flight tomorrow," Karen says.

"I'll do my best." Levi smiles. "Probably see you some time on the weekend." He pushes off the car, and takes a couple of steps back.

Karen puts the car in reverse and backs onto the street.

"Let's do this," she says.

I smile. "Bring it!"

We crank the music, and head to the highway, turning

north when we reach the traffic lights. Karen merges onto the motorway, and I settle into my seat, so ready to take a break from everything and have some fun. The drive to Surfers Paradise is more than eight hundred kilometres, and around nine hours non-stop driving time, so we're aiming for Coffs Harbour today, which is roughly halfway.

The drive is pretty non-eventful. We spend the hours chatting about the year, what we've been through, how we think we went on exams, what uni we'd like to go to, and all the usual boring stuff.

"Have you told your parents yet?" Karen asks.

"You mean about doing a fine arts degree?" I shake my head. "No. Mum will freak. She keeps telling me how I'm so smart I can do anything. I'm not sure 'artist' is on her list."

"What about Bill? He's always been pretty supportive of anything you've wanted to do."

"Yeah, but I reckon he'll take Mum's side."

We both go quiet. For a while we don't talk, and sing along to the music at the top of our lungs instead. I love Karen for not pressing me about anything to do with Levi. And I love her even more for knowing me well enough to be able to tell that I don't want to talk about him.

"So ... What do you want to do this week?" Karen asks.

"Lie on the beach," I say. "With my journal and a good book."

"We should go shopping, too," Karen says. "And eat as much ice cream as we can."

"I'm sure Jess and Stacey will want to go out to dinner."

"Of course." Karen glances at me and smiles. "And we

can also stay in and have a girlie night."

"Or two." I smile back.

"Or three ... if you want."

Karen knows that's exactly what I'd prefer over going to dinner or out to a nightclub. I was the last of us to turn eighteen, so now we're all legal, I'm pretty sure there will be one or two nights where the four of us will go dancing. I think I'm looking forward to it, but I'm also looking forward to chilling out.

We stop at Taree for a quick lunch, and to switch drivers. Karen uses the fuel card her parents gave us to fill up the car, and we get back on the road. Around three hours later we arrive in Coffs, and Karen uses Google Maps for directions to the caravan park where Mum and Dad booked us a cabin.

It isn't much, but it's a bed. After a quick call to our parents, we grab dinner from a Chinese takeaway across the street, and have a picnic on the floor in the cabin. There's not much on TV, so Karen logs on to Netflix on her phone, and we huddle together on the lounge.

I rest my head on her shoulder, and stare at the phone screen, but don't really see what's playing on it.

"Do you think things will ever work themselves out?" I ask.

Karen rests her head on top of mine. "You mean with Levi?" She takes a deep breath. "I think you've known each other far too long to give up now. Yes, the guy can be a dick, but I do believe he cares about you."

I sigh. "Sometimes he has a funny way of showing it."

"Guys are idiots."

I laugh. "Yeah."

We watch the screen for a while until the show stops. I yawn and sit up to stretch, then yawn again.

"We should go to bed," Karen says, standing. "More driving tomorrow."

I nod, but there's something I want to get off my chest first. "You know, Levi's drinking has been getting worse."

Karen stops and faces me. "I thought he only drank at parties."

I shake my head. "The fight we saw him have with his dad the other night ... I've seen it more than once. Levi blames himself for Mason's death, and I think maybe his parents do, too."

Karen sits beside me. "That's a big call."

"I know, but I just ... I want to help him."

"Well, I guess you have to try and be there for him if he needs you." She stands again. "Come on. Bedtime. Everything will look better in the morning."

I smile, because I told Levi exactly the same thing.

We go to bed, and I lie there for a while, taking slow and even breaths. We've only just left on this trip away and I'm already homesick. I want to be in my room, staring up at the glow-in-the-dark stars on my ceiling. I want to know that Levi is right next door. Instead, he's probably out drinking with his mates.

The thought of him drinking scares me, and I squeeze my eyes closed. How am I supposed to help him? For all I know it could be nothing to worry about, but my instincts are telling me otherwise.

I must fall asleep, because the next thing I know, Karen is tapping me on the shoulder, and the sun is shining through the window.

Nothing

"Let's get this party started," Karen says.

I look at her through bleary eyes. "Are you showered and dressed already?"

She grins. "In four hours we'll be soaking up the sun, sand, and surf."

"Make that five. I need to get ready." I push myself up, and swing my legs over the bed. "What time is it?"

"Seven-thirty. Now, come on." Karen grabs my arm and pulls me to my feet.

After I have a quick shower and get dressed, we throw our stuff in the car, check out, and hit the road. We pump the music and sing along at the top of our voices, and I try to enjoy the ride, but I can't help my thoughts drifting back to Levi.

I lean down and grab my phone from my bag sitting at my feet. There are no missed calls from him, or anyone. Should I call him? Maybe I should leave him alone. But now that I'm away from him, I'm not sure I want to be.

Levi will be getting on a plane soon, and he'll probably reach Surfers before us. Knowing we're both going in the same direction is comforting.

"Want me to turn the music down?" Karen yells.

"What? No." I shake my head and smile. "I'm good."

She turns it down anyway. "You going to call someone?"

I sigh. "Levi hasn't called yet." I run my finger over my phone screen, and it lights up.

"Give him a chance," Karen says. "He'll probably call tonight or tomorrow once he knows you're actually at Surfers."

"Maybe I'll call him when we get there."

"Which will be in about half an hour," Karen says.

"We just crossed the border."

"Oh. I missed the sign."

Karen smiles. "I always miss the sign."

I wind my window down to get some air on my face, and soon we're pulling into the driveway of our hotel. The concierge loads our bags onto a trolley, and Karen and I check in while the valet parks the car.

"Five-star service," I say. "Nice."

"I'll call Jess." Karen pulls her phone out, grinning. She dials Jessica's number and puts the phone to her ear. Her eyes light up. "We're here."

I can hear Jessica and Stacey squealing at the other end of the phone.

Karen hangs up, and we jump in the lift and take it to the twelfth floor where our rooms are booked. Karen squeals as she opens the door, bounding into the room, throwing her backpack and handbag onto one of the twin beds, and making a beeline for the balcony. We have an unobstructed view of the beach and the ocean, with glimpses of the streets of Surfers Paradise below. Karen's enthusiasm is infectious, and I can't help smiling.

Jessica and Stacey tumble into the room in a wave of laughter and more squealing. My cheeks hurt from smiling so much at my friends and how excited everyone is.

We ask the concierge to dump our suitcases in the wardrobe, then the four of us head downstairs and out to the strip. We have the rest of the afternoon to get our bearings before our first night begins.

Karen drags us through the shopping mall before we grab an ice cream and head for the beach. I dig my toes into the sand and stare out at the ocean. As I eat my ice cream, I think about Levi again, and I wonder for the millionth time whether he's worth all the pain. I'm like a yo-yo going up and down between loving him and hating him, and now I'm so confused.

I don't want to be angry with him anymore. I just want him. I haven't even been here a day and all I want to do is go home and spend time with him. I take a deep breath and close my eyes for a second, listening to the waves crashing on the shore, and the chatter of my friends' voices. I push Levi from my mind, and look around at my girls. I need to be in this moment with them, not thinking about a boy who has made the past few years of my life a misery.

"Earth to Katie." Karen throws a handful of sand on my legs.

"What? Did you ask me something?" I lick my ice cream to stop it running onto my hand.

"What do you want to do tonight?" she asks.

"Sitting right here sounds pretty good," Jessica says.

"We could go dancing," Stacey says. "I feel like letting loose."

I laugh. "Surfers better watch out."

Stacey also throws a handful of sand at me, a huge smile plastered on her face. "I like dancing."

"So do I," I say. "But it's our first night. Maybe we can just chill out. You know, hang out at the markets. Go for walks and feel the sand between our toes."

"Oh no. This can't be good." Karen looks past me along the beach.

I turn to see what she's looking at. Jarred and Geoff are walking along the water's edge, and I immediately look for Levi. I scan the shoreline and the sand, but I can't see him anywhere. I'm not in the mood to talk to Levi's friends, Geoff especially.

"I think I'll head back to the room for a bit." I get up and brush the sand from my shorts.

"Want us to come?" Karen asks.

"No, it's fine. I'll go call Mum and unpack a few things. Meet you when the markets start?"

"Sure." She smiles up at me, shading her eyes from the afternoon sun.

"We'll make sure the beach doesn't go anywhere," Jessica says.

I walk up the sand towards the steps leading to the strip. Jarred and Geoff look in my direction, but I keep walking. As I make my way back to the hotel, I keep an eye out for Levi, hoping to run into him, but I don't.

When I get to our room, I fuss around for a bit, unpacking some clothes and setting my toiletries up in the bathroom, making sure there's enough space for Karen as well. I wash my face to freshen up, then I go and open the sliding door and sit on the balcony.

A crisp breeze blows off the ocean, and I rub my arms, even though it's been warm today. I stare at the water, and loneliness settles into my stomach.

"Snap out of it, Katie," I mumble to myself.

I pull my phone from my pocket and call home.

Mum answers on the first ring. "Sweetie, how are you?"

"Great, Mum. The room is amazing ... thank you."

"No problems getting there?"

"No," I say. "Everything is fine."

Nothing

I put my feet up on the railing, and lean my forehead on my knees. Nothing is fine. I'm not fine. I want to go home, but fine is what you say when you're eight hundred and fifty kilometres from home, and you're supposed to be having fun.

"Okay, well, stay safe," Mum says. "Give me a call in a couple of days."

I hit End, sit back in the chair, and rub my face, then look at my phone to see what time it is. Karen, Jessica, and Stacey are expecting me to show up back at the beach in a little more than half an hour. The Friday night markets start at four o'clock, and I really want to wander through them, but now I don't feel like leaving the room.

I stare at the ocean, and try to decide what to do.

My phone buzzes in my lap with a message.

Daniel: How r u?

I sigh and write a reply.

Me: Need new word 4 fine

Daniel: Want 2 talk?

Me: No. But WYWH

Daniel: Call me later?

Me: OK

As I hit send, Levi's name flashes on the screen, and my phone buzzes out its ring tone. I blink and stare at it for a few heartbeats.

I swipe my finger across the screen. "Hey."

"Hey," Levi replies. "You get here okay?"

"Yeah. You?"

"All good. No hassles."

"Our room is really nice. You should see it."

"Maybe you can show me later." I hear the smile in

his voice, and I smile as well.

I pick at the edge of the chair handle and stare down at the beach, wondering if Levi is walking along it. The sun will be setting soon, and the reflection through the clouds has set the sky ablaze.

"Where are you?" I ask. "Can you see the water?"

"No. I'm at the pub. The boys and I are having a beer."

"Oh." I go quiet for a moment. "Well, the ocean looks beautiful. And the sky is amazing." I stare at the red and pink tones seeping into the clouds. "Even though the sun doesn't set over the water, it looks like the show will be good."

"Want to sit on the beach at sunset tomorrow night?"

My breath catches, and I open my mouth then close it again. "I'd love to, but I'm not sure what the girls want to do."

Levi is quiet on the other end of the phone. Then he says, "I miss you, Katie."

What am I supposed to tell him? I miss him, too, but I feel like I can't breathe. Still, this might be my opportunity to move forward. Is it time to let Levi do the breathing for me?

"I'll be down at the markets soon," I say. "Maybe we'll run into each other."

"Yeah, okay. I'll look for you." Levi says, his voice sounding happier. "I'll see you later?"

"Bye."

The phone goes dead, and I smile, staring at the screen until it blinks off. The sun is lower, and I check the time. I'm surprised Karen hasn't called to see where I am. I quickly text her to let her know I'm on my way. My phone buzzes a few seconds after I hit send.

Karen: Meet U at mall entrance

Me: OK

I grab my cardigan and purse, lock the room on my way out, and head for the lift. I stare at my reflection in the mirror as the lift takes me to the lobby, and I smile again.

Maybe for the next few days I can pretend I don't have any problems, or baggage. I'm not the poor girl. I'm not the girl everyone goes out of their way to embarrass. And I'm not the girl who has had her heart broken by the boy next door more than once.

I'm the girl who's ready to open her eyes, and start living again.

9

What I'm looking for

When I get back to the foreshore, I walk through the markets and glance around quickly as I make my way towards the pedestrian lights across from the entrance to the mall. All sorts of items are on display, from brightly coloured artworks, to knitted hats, and tie-dyed sarongs. I snort. There's even a stall where you can get your fortune read.

I find Karen, Jessica, and Stacey near the lights.

"Did you see the fortune teller?" Karen says, grabbing my arm.

"Yes." I raise my eyebrows. "Why?"

"You should totally get a reading."

I bite my bottom lip. "No way."

"It could be fun." Stacey shrugs.

"You could ask about Levi," Jessica says.

Nothing

"Yes, yes, yes." Karen jumps up and down, still clutching me. "You could find out what's going to happen between you two."

I laugh. "You don't seriously believe that stuff, do you?"

"Come on, Katie," Karen says. "Lighten up. We're here to have fun."

"Then why don't you get your fortune told?" I ask.

"Me? I'm boring. I have no love life." She pulls me back into the markets and towards the fortune-teller stall. "You're far more interesting."

We stop outside the small tent. There's an A-frame sign on the right advertising 'Fortune Telling by Madame Leora'. The marquee is draped in purple fabric on all sides, with the panels at the front pulled aside and fixed to the poles like curtains. Attached to the fabric around the door is a variety of dried flowers, and herbs. Trinkets, beads, and crystals hang in strings in the open space.

"Looks cute." Stacey touches the fabric.

"And creepy," Jessica says.

Karen pushes me towards the threshold of the stall, and I part the beaded curtain to gaze around at the inside. The floor is covered with a Persian-look rug. Paper lanterns hang from the fabric ceiling. There's a small table in the centre with flickering candles on it, and a tarot deck set to one side.

A woman dressed in a black lace dress, purple headscarf, and with heavy eye make-up stares at me from one of the two seats at the table. She leans forward and rests her hands on the wood in front of her. Her bangles and the several rings on her fingers clink with her movement.

"Welcome," she says in a low, husky voice. "I am Madame Leora. What is it you wish to know?"

I stare at her, then whisper to Karen, "I don't think this is a good idea."

"Come on." Karen nudges me towards the empty chair. "Katie would like her fortune told. How much?"

No beating around the bush then.

"Twenty-five dollars per reading," Madame Leora says. "Forty for two."

"Here." Karen hands over the money.

I glance at Jessica then Stacey, and they both shrug. With a sigh, I pull the chair out and sit at the table. I make a note to buy Karen something this week. I don't want to waste her money, but who knows? I might find out something interesting.

"Only the subject can be in here," Madame Leora says.

Karen folds her arms. "Why?"

"We can't have any outside influences. If you want to stay, it's another fifteen dollars, and I will read the cards for you, too."

"Okay. We'll come back in half an hour." Karen ushers Jessica and Stacey out of the stall.

I watch the beads and crystals fall back into place, then turn to face Madame Leora.

"I've never done this before." I twist my fingers together in my lap.

"Relax," she says. "It will help us get a more accurate reading. Are you ready?"

I take a deep breath and let it out slowly, shake my hands, and put them on the table, then nod. "How does this work?"

Madame Leora picks up the tarot deck. "First, we need to clear the deck to remove all the energy from the last reading, and attune the cards to you." She hands me the deck. "Shuffle them. Then hold them with both hands, and close your eyes. Visualise a bright white light extending from your fingers and into the cards."

Okay then.

I do as I'm told, sitting up straight and shuffling the cards, flipping them clumsily between my hands. Then I clutch them tightly. With my eyes closed, I try and picture whiteness surrounding me. I feel like an idiot, but I'm strangely calm.

Madame Leora says, "Open your eyes. Now you need to ask your question."

"How do I do that?" I stare at her, my fingers gripping the cards.

"Ask your question in your mind." She nods at me. "Go on."

I adjust my hold around the deck of cards, and stare at them. What am I going to ask? What do I *really* want to know? I can't ask if Levi loves me, because I already know he does, although he has a weird way of showing it. I want to know if we have a future together, but I also want to know if that future will work out. Will everything be okay between us? Will we be happy? Or will all our problems get in the way? I don't want a future with him if that future is bleak.

Then I think of a question that seems almost too perfect, and exactly what I want to find an answer for.

Will Levi and I be able to find forgiveness?

It seems forgiveness is the one thing both of us are

seeking, whether it's from each other, or from ourselves. And I'm hoping that with forgiveness will come happiness.

"Okay, I have my question." I look up.

"Good." Madame Leora places her hands over mine and leans forward. "Now, channel that question into the cards."

I stare down at my hands again, and take a deep breath. *This isn't going to work, surely.* Fortune telling is ridiculous. But I want an answer to my question more than anything.

Madame Leora takes the deck from my grasp and places it on the table. "Split the cards with your left hand."

My fingers shake as I reach for the cards, taking half the deck and placing it to the left side of the pile. "Now what?"

Madame Leora puts the two piles of cards back together. "Now we see what the cards have to say." She places the first three cards face down in a line on the table in front of me. "Turn each card over, starting from my left. The first card represents your past. The middle is where you are now, and the third is what your future may give you."

I hold my breath, my hand hovering over the first card, eager to find out what the cards will say, but completely scared at the same time. I pinch the edge of the card and turn it over. A knight in silver armour, sitting on a white horse and holding a black and white flag, stares up at me.

"Death," Madame Leora says.

"That doesn't sound good," I mumble.

"You have had a sudden change in your past. Someone close to you instigated this change, but you must not dwell. Because where one door closes, another opens."

Nothing

I stare at Madame Leora and crinkle my nose. Really? She's using that old cliché? But then I think about it for a second. Levi was close to me, and he instigated a big change in my life. He ended our friendship. Killed it. Maybe the death card is pretty spot on.

With a deep breath, I grab the middle card and turn it over. A man, looking like the pope and holding a sceptre, stares at me.

"The Hierophant," Madame Leora says.

"The what?" This is so bogus. Why am I even here?

"Recently, you have come to terms with doing what is expected of you, even when you have not wanted to." Madame Leora's voice is becoming huskier. The flames from the candles on the table flicker in her eyes. "You have been wise in conforming. It has led you to great achievements."

I bite my lip. Does she mean becoming dux? I can't think of any other great achievements in my life, and I was pretty much forced to do what everyone expected the day I won my scholarship. Now, I want to pursue a career in the arts. That's not exactly conforming to my parents' wishes.

I pick up the third card. My fingers slip, and another card drops to the table, landing face down. Were they stuck together?

Madame Leora presses her fingertips together. I still have the third card in my hand.

"What? What does this mean?" I ask, my fingers trembling.

"Put the card on the table." She lays her hands in front of her and spreads her fingers. "We will worry about the fourth card in a minute."

I put the third card down beside the middle one. A man in a black cloak stands with five cups at his feet. Three of them have been knocked over.

"What's this one?" I ask.

"The five of cups." Madame Leora looks at me. "You are feeling disappointed, and you're having trouble letting go of your past." She points to the death card. "You need to find forgiveness, whether it be for someone else or yourself. It is not until you can learn to forgive that you will find happiness."

My mouth drops open. Then I snap it shut. Did she know my question? How has she been able to read the cards to mirror exactly what has happened to me, and what I've been thinking?

It has to be a generic response to whatever card gets turned. *What a load of crap.* It's a coincidence this card has come up and this weirdo has said what she's said. I stare down at the cards in disbelief, and a wave of cold rushes through me.

This is totally creeping me out.

"Turn the fourth card," Madame Leora says.

I don't want to. But I slip my fingernail under it anyway and turn it over, placing it beside the five of cups. A tower sits on top of a mountain. Lightning strikes the tip of it, and flames billow from the windows.

"This doesn't look good either," I say. It would take an idiot not to see that.

"The tower," Madame Leora says. "You will face great turmoil. Something unexpected and tragic lies ahead. You will be tested in your ability to forgive. You need to be prepared." The psychic sits back, and regards me for a moment. She doesn't say anything else.

"That's it?" I ask. "My future holds something tragic and unexpected? Could you be more vague?"

"I just read the cards," she says. "Now, you need to close the reading. Pick them up and place them back in the pack, please."

I stare at her with my mouth agape before scoffing and sweeping the cards together. "Okay, then." I get up from the chair and go to the curtained door, then turn to face Madame Leora. "How much of this should I believe?"

Madame Leora stacks the cards on the table near the candles. "As much as your heart can manage." She stares at me, and I turn away, parting the beads and stepping out into the markets. "I hope you find what you're looking for," she calls after me.

I hesitate for a second, hugging my purse to my chest. Nothing she said could possibly be true. It's all a hoax. A pre-written script designed to apply to pretty much every person ever. But so much of what Madame Leora said is close to … everything. A shiver runs down my spine, partly because of the outcome of my fortune telling, and partly because Levi is standing across from me.

Maybe I've already found what I'm looking for.

Still standing

I stare at Levi as a trickle of people walk between us. He has his hands shoved into his jeans pockets, and is wearing a nice shirt, as if he's ready to go out on the town. Of course he is. He's probably going to hit the nightclubs later with his mates.

I'm still wearing the shorts and singlet top I threw on this morning when Karen and I left Coffs Harbour. Was that really this morning? It feels like a million years ago, and I stifle a yawn.

Levi comes towards me, dodging a few people to cross the main thoroughfare of the markets. I glance around to see if I can find Karen and the others, but they're nowhere in sight. I look back to Levi and smile.

"Fortune telling?" he asks when he reaches me.

"Yeah. It was ... totally a waste of money." I chew on

my bottom lip, and look around again.

"What's wrong?" Levi shifts on his feet.

"Sorry ... I'm just looking for Karen."

"Call her." Levi shrugs. "She's probably checking out the stalls."

I open my purse and take my phone out to text Karen instead.

Me: Finished. Will look at stalls then B on beach

Karen is quick to reply.

Karen: Jess getting a tatt

What? I stare at the screen with my mouth open, then another message comes through.

Karen: Don't panic not real

Karen: Henna

I smile then laugh, because for a second, I did panic. Besides, if any of my friends are going to get a tattoo, I want to be there.

"What's so funny?" Levi asks.

I put my phone away. "Jess is getting henna. Karen was trying to freak me out, that's all."

Levi smiles and pulls his hands from his pockets, running one of them through his hair. My insides flip, and I smile wider because he still has this effect on me.

"What did the fortune teller say?" Levi asks.

I shake my head and look up at him. "Nothing important. Or true."

I clutch my purse, and fiddle with the zipper pull, not sure what else to say or what to talk about.

"Hey, Levi," someone yells.

Levi turns towards the voice. I look around him to see who it is. Jarred and Geoff are walking towards us.

"Come on," Jarred says. "We want another beer."

"Or two, or three." Geoff grins.

I scrunch my nose up. I can't believe Levi is friends with him. I'm not about to tell him who he can and can't be friends with though.

Levi faces me again. "What are you doing tonight?"

I look up and down the stalls. "Shopping, and I'll probably sit on the beach for a bit."

"What about tomorrow? Want to have lunch with me?"

Geoff snickers. "Dude. Beer. Let's go."

I glare at him, then make eye contact with Levi. "You should go be with your friends."

"Yeah, but I'd really like to spend some time with you."

"Can I call you? I'll check what the girls are up to. I don't want to ditch them."

Levi backs away a few steps, nodding. "Okay." He turns and walks with his two mates into the crowd.

I let out a long breath. Is it ever going to be easy to be around Levi? To talk to him normally again like I used to when we were younger? I don't know why I'm finding it so hard now. Actually, I do.

It's a trust thing.

And a forgiveness thing.

Like Madame Leora said. I need to find forgiveness.

I shiver again, and move away from the fortune-telling stall without looking back. I should never have gone in there. Not that I *really* believe any of it, but a horrible feeling has settled into my stomach since I left that tent. To try and shake it, I walk the stalls for a bit, stopping at a stand where a pretty girl with a nose ring is selling her artworks. They are all beautiful black ink drawings with splashes of colour. A unicorn catches my eye. Its mane and tail are painted in a rainbow. I love the magical feel to it, so I pay the artist, tuck the small artwork into my purse, and move on to the next stall.

The hum of voices around me is soothing, and I get lost in the crowd for a while. I don't buy anything else, but I enjoy looking at everything and forcing myself not to think about anything other than exactly what I'm doing right now.

Eventually, I end up on the beach where I'd told Karen I was going. I pull my phone out and send her a message

Me: On beach now

Karen: C U soon

I walk towards the ocean, sitting and kicking my shoes off so I can sink my toes into the cool sand. I move them back and forth, concentrating on the feeling of the grains running over my skin.

I prop my elbows on my knees, and listen to the waves pounding against the shore. The noise from the markets hums behind me, and I breathe in a deep breath, holding it for a few heartbeats before slowly letting it out. I close my eyes, and my thoughts immediately go to Levi. Forgiveness is hard to find, but I want it so badly.

"There you are." Karen drops onto the sand beside me. "How did the reading go?"

Jessica and Stacey flop onto the sand as well, their faces all smiles.

"Yes! Tell us," Stacey says.

I look at Jessica's hand. "Show me your tatt first."

She giggles, but holds out her arm. "It's henna. Not permanent."

"It's beautiful." I look closely at the swirls and dots marking her skin in a light brown ink.

Jessica drops her arm. "You should get one."

"Maybe later," I say.

"We could all get one done," Stacey says.

Voices drift to us along the beach, broken by the sound of the waves crashing on the shore. I spot a group of people sitting in the sand at the base of the steps leading up to the markets, about a hundred metres away.

"So, the reading?" Karen asks.

"It was totally bogus." I stare in the direction of the other voices. "I reckon they work to a script and tell everyone the same thing, depending on which cards get turned over."

"It must have been more exciting than that," Stacey says.

I laugh. "It wasn't."

"Should we go back to the room?" Jessica says. "We could curl up and eat chocolate and watch TV."

"It's our first night," Stacey says. "We should go and have some fun."

"We should get some sleep," Jessica says. "We have plenty of time. And I think Katie and Karen are pretty tired after driving for two days to get here."

"I'm good with chocolate and TV," Karen says.

I smile at her. "You guys go ahead. I want to sit and listen to the ocean. I'll come back in an hour."

Jessica gets up and brushes the sand from her shorts. "You'll be okay by yourself?"

"Sure." I nod. "It's a five-minute walk to the hotel."

Stacey sighs and gets to her feet as well. "You guys

promise we can go dancing tomorrow night?" She reaches down and pulls Karen up.

"Let's just see what happens," I say.

"That's a yes." Stacey jumps up and down and claps her hands. The rest of us giggle at how silly she looks.

"That's a maybe." I smile at my friends.

Jessica and Stacey make their way back towards the strip.

Karen looks down at me. "You won't be long?"

"No." I shake my head, loving that she knows exactly when not to push me, or ask if I'm okay. I'm pretty sick of that question.

"See you back at the room." She walks backwards a few steps in the sand. "An hour ... then I'm coming to look for you."

"I'll text you when I'm on my way." I smile.

Karen turns and joins our other two friends, and I watch them until they're up on the footpath and walking towards the hotel. The voices up the beach drift to me again, and I face their direction, digging my toes deeper into the sand. They sound so happy. I could use some happiness right now, but I don't move.

I need this time to think. I don't want to talk to anyone. I just want to listen to the water, and stare at the huge vastness of the ocean. Be swallowed by the nothingness, and maybe find a single moment of peace.

Sand flicks into the air and lands on my legs as someone sits down beside me.

"Nice night, isn't it?"

I look at the guy. He's cute and has nice eyes. He stretches his legs out in front of him and grins, then leans back on one hand and sifts sand through his fingers with the other.

"Yes." I hug my knees to my chest and stare at the water. "It is."

"Where you from?"

I look at him again. "Sydney. You?"

The guy flicks his head to shake his blond hair from his eyes. "Same. I'm from the Shire."

I chuckle. "Sydney is a big place. I live on the North Shore."

"Cool," the guy says. He stares at me. "What's your name?"

I hesitate before saying, "Katie."

"Well, pleased to meet you, Katie. I'm Scott." He sits up and sifts more sand through his fingers. "We're having a party up the beach if you want to join us."

"Yes, I can hear the noise," I say. "Maybe later." I don't really want to move from my quiet spot.

Scott gets to his feet and brushes the sand from his hands. "No problem. Hope to see you again." He gives me a wink.

I'm not used to this sort of attention from guys, so I'm not sure how to respond. I opt for a smile and a wave as he walks away. Levi is the only one who has ever offered me any sort of romantic attention. Scott is cute, and he seems nice enough, but he's not Levi.

I watch Scott's back as he makes his way along the beach towards the small but noisy group of people, and I can't help wondering how long it will be until the cops come and break up their little party.

I wriggle my toes in the sand. I should go back to the

hotel and find my girls, and I stand to do just that when I hear someone call my name. I search the faces I can make out and find Veronica waving at me. She's standing a little way away from the edge of the main party group.

"Katie, come over," she says.

I glance towards the direction of the hotel, and then at Veronica again. I guess I could talk to her for a few minutes. I lean down to scoop my thongs and purse up before making my way towards her and the party.

"Hey," I say when I reach her, glancing around at all the unfamiliar faces. "Good party?"

"Nothing like the ones we have back home." She laughs.

I press my lips together, then laugh with her. "So you haven't truth or dared anyone yet?"

She shrugs. "All they're interested in is drinking."

"And you don't want to?"

"I'm not stupid. Especially after ..."

Veronica's unfinished words hang between us, and I get the feeling she's thinking about what Geoff tried to do to her.

She toes the sand. "But we don't need to talk about that."

"Is the rest of your group here?" I ask to change the subject.

"Geoff is around somewhere. Rachel is sitting on the steps." She points, and I follow her hand to halfway up the stairs. "Levi, Jarred, and Josie are I-have-no-idea-where. We left them at the pub."

Veronica moves, and I see Scott behind her. Our eyes connect.

"Katie, you came over," he says, walking towards us.

"Want a drink?"

"Um ... no thanks, I'm good," I say.

"Come and meet my friends then." Scott backs away before turning and walking to the far left of the steps.

"I'll catch up with you later," Veronica says, looking at Scott, then back to me and smiling.

"Sure," I say, my thongs dangling from my fingers.

Veronica joins Rachel on the steps. I should go back to the hotel, but I'm here now. I guess meeting some new people won't hurt. I'm here to have fun, and apart from Veronica, and Rachel, I can't see anyone I know. The thought comforts me. It's the perfect opportunity to be whoever I want to be.

Scott introduces me to a few people, and their names blur together. There's no way I'm going to remember them, so I don't even try. I take a quick look around. Veronica said Geoff was here, but I haven't seen him yet.

I settle into the sand, planning to stay for ten minutes, but time gets on as I fall into a conversation with a nice girl named Mia. Scott inches closer to me with every beer he has, and I think it's time for me to leave.

I get to my feet, and wipe my sandy palms on my shorts.

"Are you going to uni?" Scott asks, jumping up to stand beside me.

"I'd like to." I don't elaborate. I want to get away and go back to the hotel.

"What do you want to do?" Mia asks.

I want to be an artist, but that probably won't happen.

"I have no idea." I don't want to get into it with these strangers, so I reach down to grab my purse and thongs. "I'm going to call it a night. It was nice meeting you.

Maybe I'll run into you guys later."

Before any of them can protest, I head up the beach, planning to walk the sand until the last set of stairs. After sitting amongst the loud chatter, I want some quiet.

"Katie, wait," Scott says from behind me. "Don't go yet."

"I'm tired." I turn and take a couple of backwards steps before continuing.

I quicken my pace, aware Scott is following me. This end of the beach is almost deserted. Fear rises into my belly, being so far away from other people with a guy I don't know. I turn and head for the closest set of stairs that will take me onto the road and towards people and traffic.

Scott grabs my arm. "Come on. I thought we could have some fun tonight."

"Let go of me." I yank my arm free and walk a few more steps.

Scott jogs past me, then stands in my path. "What is it with you girls? We're at schoolies."

I glare at him. "And you think that means someone you just met is going to put out?"

Scott steps towards me. He stands so close his breath brushes my face. It smells like stale beer, and it makes me want to gag.

"You only live once. I say you have to grab every opportunity with both hands."

I take a step backwards and stumble. Scott locks his hands around my upper arms and stops me falling. He yanks me towards him, and holds me tightly against his chest with one arm. Bile rises into my throat. He caresses my cheek with his free hand, then runs his fingertips down to my collarbone before wrapping his hand around my throat.

My purse and thongs fall to the sand as I reach up and try to free his grip.

"Get off me!" I shove him as hard as I can, but it makes no difference.

"Come on, Katie." He holds me tighter, his thumb pressing into my windpipe.

"Please," I manage to force out as I wriggle in his grasp. "Let go."

I struggle for a few more heartbeats, then I settle. It's obvious I'm not going to get out of this with pure strength. I relax in Scott's arms, and stare into his eyes. They're glassy, and I'm pretty sure he's drunker than I've ever seen Levi.

"That's better." He relaxes his grip, then leans in.

I turn my head to the side as he tries to kiss me, suddenly very aware of how Veronica must have felt.

"Please," I say again. "I have a boyfriend."

Scott laughs. "Where is he then? What he doesn't know won't hurt him."

How do I get out of this? I need to distract him.

"You're right," I say, turning to look into Scott's eyes. "He's not here, so I guess there's no harm in fooling around."

Scott smiles, and he moves his hand onto my shoulder. I have to stop myself gulping air, taking an even breath instead. I smile back at him, and wait for him to loosen his hold a little more. Finally, he does, leaning in to kiss me again, and I take the opportunity to pull my leg back.

Then I knee him in the balls.

Scott lets go of me and doubles over. "You bitch," he chokes out.

Nothing

I push him away and try to go back towards the party, but he grabs my arm. We're too far away from anyone to hear me if I yell. I glance up the beach and spot a group of people walking towards us, but it's too dark to make out any of their faces. If they come close enough maybe Scott will leave me alone. I fight to pull my arm free, and the image of Veronica fighting Geoff enters my head. I remember standing there with the toilet brush, and I laugh.

"What's so funny?" Scott asks.

"You're a drunk idiot." I try to pull away again, but he grabs me around the waist and yanks me to his chest. "Get off me! I'll kick you again."

From the corner of my eye I see someone running towards us.

"Hey!" he yells. "Leave her alone."

I twist in Scott's arms and break free.

The guy grabs Scott and rips him away from me. The two boys tumble to the sand and roll over each other.

My mouth drops open when I see it's Geoff who has tackled Scott. Geoff pulls his arm back and slogs Scott in the face.

I look around, and Veronica is here with Rachel.

"Katie?" Veronica says. "Are you all right?"

I open and close my mouth a few times, staring at the people I thought I hated the most, but who have come to my rescue. Scott gets to his feet, and Geoff shoves him before he's fully upright. He lands heavily in the sand.

"Who's this guy?" Geoff asks.

"He was at the party over there." I point to where we'd been on the beach.

Geoff kicks sand at Scott. "Get lost, before I make you."

"She was asking for it." Scott scrambles to his feet and staggers along the beach, back towards his friends.

Veronica puts her hand on my arm. "Did he do anything to you?"

I shake my head and rub my neck. "Just grabbed me."

Rachel doesn't say anything. I'm grateful, because I will probably burst into tears if she does.

I look at Veronica. "Thanks, for … you know …?"

"I know." She hugs me, and at first, I'm not sure what to do. Then I lift my arms and hug her back. "I figure I owe you," she says softly.

"Come on, guys," Rachel says. "Katie's fine. Let's go."

Veronica pulls away from me.

I retrieve my purse and thongs from where I dropped them. "I'm heading back to the hotel now anyway."

"Want me to walk with you?" Veronica asks.

"I can walk her," Geoff says.

I frown at him. "I'm good."

"We'll catch up later then?" Veronica and Rachel link arms and head off together.

I nod then walk to the steps, because continuing up the dark beach alone is not a good idea after what just happened. When I reach the top stair I stop, slip my thongs on, and turn to look back at the waves. Veronica and Rachel are walking along the sand, but Geoff is standing at the bottom of the stairs looking up at me.

He takes the steps two at a time until he's a couple down from me. "You should let me walk you."

I laugh, even though it's not funny. "I'm a big girl. I can look after myself."

"Really? What would you have done if we hadn't shown

up tonight?"

"What would Veronica have done if I hadn't been there at the formal?"

He frowns, then glances at his feet before meeting my eyes again. "For what it's worth, I know I'm a dick. Especially when I'm drunk."

"Yeah, you can say that again." I press my lips together. "It's no excuse."

He nods. "You're right. What I did to Ronnie was … unforgiveable. And I'm glad you stopped me. I would've hated myself in the morning."

"Veronica would've hated you more."

Geoff walks up the remaining stairs and stands beside me. "Come on, Katie. Levi would kill me if I let anything happen to you."

I frown, and stare at him for a moment. "Let's go then."

I don't completely trust Geoff, but we fall into step beside each other.

"Why did you help me?" I ask as we walk. "I'm the last person you'd want to be seen with."

Geoff scratches his head and shoves one hand in his pocket. "I guess it's my way of apologising for … you know … everything. You said it yourself. We could all use a new beginning."

I chew the side of my thumb, not sure what to say. One thing I do know is that I'm tired of people saying sorry to me. Don't do something in the first place that requires an apology, and everyone will be so much happier.

"I'm not sure I can give you that. I don't trust you, or like you very much."

"That's okay. If I were you, I wouldn't like me either."

We stop outside the hotel. "This is me. Thanks."

"No problem. Maybe I'll see you around this week," Geoff says.

"Maybe." I walk into the hotel and don't look back.

Inside, I suck in a deep breath and take my phone out of my purse. I have five missed calls from Karen. When I get to our room, Karen, Stacey, and Jessica are all waiting.

"Where have you been?" Karen pounces on me. "You didn't text me. I was about to come find you."

I look at my phone screen. The door clicks shut behind me. "I'm ten minutes late. I met some people on the beach. Lost track of time."

I'm not about to tell them what really happened. I'd rather forget the whole night, what with the creepy tarot reading, getting assaulted, and then Geoff helping me. I should have come back with my friends.

Or kneed Scott in the balls harder.

"Everything all right?" Jessica asks.

"Yeah." I nod. "I'm tired though. Think I'll call it a night."

"We could probably all use a good night's sleep," Karen says.

Jessica and Stacey hug me before going next door to their room. Karen gives me a hug, too, and I go into the bathroom to wash my face. I stare at the mirror, and I smile at myself, because despite everything I've been through, I'm still standing.

You have to choose

We all sleep in the next morning, and it's nice not having to get up for anything in particular, or be anywhere special. The four of us spend the day lazing by the pool at the hotel, soaking up some sun. We have a light lunch on the beach, and I enjoy walking along the sand.

I told Levi I would call him, but I've been putting it off because spending time with my friends right now is exactly what I need. I text him to say maybe we can do lunch another time. He doesn't reply, and it's not until my phone rings late in the afternoon that I feel a little guilty for not calling him instead. Still, I stare at Levi's name flashing on the screen and let it ring out. After last night and what happened with Scott, maybe I should swear off boys forever. I'm yet to meet one who hasn't hurt me, not including Daniel and Dad of course. But then, Levi isn't Scott.

"You don't want to talk to him?" Karen asks, linking her arm through mine as we walk up the beach.

"I don't know what I want," I say. "And I have no idea what to do."

"Maybe now is when you need to give him a second chance."

I squeeze Karen's arm. "Maybe. But not today." I slip my phone into my back pocket. "Today I want to be with you."

We spend the rest of the afternoon and night at the hotel. Jessica and Stacey go out dancing for a couple of hours, but they're home and on the couch with Karen and me by ten pm. My friends must sense I'm not in the mood to party, and I'm grateful to have their company.

The next two days go pretty much the same. Jessica and Stacey do their own thing for a few hours at night, and Karen keeps me company either on the beach, or back in our room. We gaze at the stars together, and talk about life and what we want to do when we grow up.

Levi calls every day.

But I don't answer.

Now it's six-thirty pm, and I'm looking at another night on the couch because I don't feel like going anywhere. I hear my phone ring, and when I come out of the bathroom, Karen is staring at me. She has my phone in her hand.

"What?" I ask. "Why are you looking at me like that?"

"This has gone on long enough," she says. "We've been here for five days, and all you've done is mope in our hotel room, and walk on the beach."

"That's not true." I twist my finger into the hem of my

top. "I had my fortune told."

"Yeah, which you haven't given me any details about. Come on, Katie." Karen stands. "Tomorrow we should go and get some henna done. Or have a drink in one of the bars tonight."

"I don't want to drink."

She drops her hands to her sides. "I spoke to Levi. He wants to see you."

"What happened to you hating him for what he did to me?"

Karen walks towards me and wraps me up in a hug. "I do hate him for what he did. But I know you, and I know you're trying to figure out a way to forgive him. Because he's Levi." She pulls back and smiles.

Tears sting my eyes, and then they're spilling onto my cheeks faster than I can wipe them away. "I'm so confused," I say between sobs. "What if I forgive him and he hurts me again? What if—"

"You won't know unless you try." Karen strokes my hair. "You don't want to spend the rest of your life wondering 'what if', do you?"

I look at my best friend, and take a deep breath, shaking my head. "I'm scared."

"Not knowing what will happen is part of the fun." She smiles.

I laugh, because so far none of this has been 'fun'.

"What did he say to you?" I ask.

Karen hands me my phone. "He wants to take you to dinner. We have a few days left before we have to go home. Just ... go and see him."

I take my phone and look down at it. "Okay."

Karen goes into the bathroom, and I sit on the edge of the couch, squeezing my knees together. My fingers hover over the screen of my phone, then I key in my passcode. Levi is at the top of my most recent calls list. It looks like he spoke to Karen for a few minutes.

After a moment of hesitation, I hit Levi's name and hold the phone to my ear.

He answers on the second ring.

"Katie, hi."

"Hey," I say. "Karen said you called."

I wince at my stupid words, since I've been ignoring his calls for the past few days.

"So she convinced you to call me back?"

Silence hangs between us, and I bite my lip. This is harder than it should be. "Yeah."

"Did she also tell you she said she'd rip my balls off if I hurt you again?" He laughs.

I cough and stand. "She said what?"

Levi's laugh intensifies.

Karen comes out of the bathroom, and our gazes meet. "Did you threaten to rip Levi's balls off?"

Karen raises her eyebrows and smiles. "I sure did."

I shake my head and walk onto the balcony, leaning on the railing. There's still some light left in the sky even though the sun has gone down. The stars twinkle above, and I watch them blink in the hazy darkness.

"What've you been doing?" I finally ask.

"The usual." Levi pauses. "Hanging out. You?"

"Same. Pool. Beach. Chocolate in front of the TV." I close my eyes and shake my head. *I'm so lame.*

"Want to grab something to eat tonight?" Levi asks.

Nothing

"Um … Okay. What time?" I ask.

"Now," Levi says.

"You'll have to give me a chance to get ready."

"You're beautiful exactly how you are." I hear the smile in his voice. "Look down, Katie."

My chest warms at him telling me I'm beautiful. I drag my gaze away from the sky and look to the street. Levi is standing on the other side of the road, his face tilted up towards me.

"How did you know …?" I adjust the phone at my ear.

"Karen told me which hotel you're staying at. I just spotted you."

I press my lips together. "Give me ten minutes." Then I end the call.

Levi pulls his phone from his ear before I go back inside. Karen is standing in the middle of the room holding up a summer dress. My one pair of nice sandals hang from her fingers.

"Better change quickly," she says.

"Not that dress," I say. "It looks amazing on you. Me … not so much."

I dig around in my case until I find my three-quarter jeans and paisley top. Karen sighs, but doesn't say anything as I tug off my shorts and change. I set my glasses on the coffee table while I run a comb through my hair.

"Don't you want to put your contacts in?" Karen asks.

"No time," I say. "And if he likes me, he has to like everything about me. Glasses included."

"You're testing him."

"I guess." I shrug. "But you know how long it takes me to put those things in. I really don't have time."

Karen hands me my purse, and I slip my phone inside after quickly coating my lips with gloss. I grab one of the room keys on the way to the door. As I step into the hall, Jessica and Stacey's door opens.

Stacey looks me up and down, smiling. "Where you going?"

"She has a date with Levi," Karen says.

"Finally." Jessica comes out to the hallway.

"Call me if you need us," Karen says. "I'll text you and let you know where we end up."

I smile and back away before turning to head towards the lifts. My hand shakes as I reach out to press the button. Why am I so nervous? I've known Levi my whole life, and there's pretty much nothing he doesn't know about me. I get into the lift and press the button for the ground floor.

When I step out into the lobby, Levi is waiting. A smile spreads across his face, and I can't help smiling back. I clutch my purse to my chest like a shield, and walk over to him.

"You look great, Katie," he says.

"Thanks." Heat prickles my cheeks, and I resist the urge to touch my glasses, gripping my purse tighter instead.

"What do you feel like eating?" he asks, walking towards the front doors of the hotel.

I fall into step beside him. "Anything. I don't mind."

"Let's hit the mall and see what we can find."

We step out into the balmy night air, and walk down to the foreshore. It gets busier as we get nearer to the mall, and the hum of activity wafts along the street. We walk in silence for a bit, and I listen to the crashing of the waves on the beach. It's dark enough now that I can't see the water from the strip, but I turn my face in that direction anyway.

"Can we go down to the beach later?" I ask. "I like listening to the waves."

"Anything you want," Levi says.

I smile at him.

We keep walking, and I people watch. Couples out like us. Larger groups of friends. People on pushbikes and skateboards. There's activity everywhere.

We stop at the lights to cross the road into the mall. When the little man turns green, Levi takes my hand. I look up at him and smile. He leads me through the mall to the pub, and while I said I don't mind what we eat, I'm not sure I want to eat here. Still, I go with it, and a few minutes later we're seated together in a booth up the back.

It's noisy, with groups of people filling most of the seats, and every stool at the bar is taken. A waitress in a short black skirt and tight white button blouse sashays over to us, a notepad in her hand.

"What can I get yas?" she says, her bright red lips turning up into a wide smile.

I pick up the menu from the table and quickly scan it.

"I'll have the steak burger," Levi says, without looking at what's on offer.

I bite my lip and flip the menu over, then back again. The meals look big, and I'm not very hungry.

"Wedges, thanks." I look up at the waitress, but she's ogling Levi.

"Drinks?" Miss Flirty asks.

I frown, and glance at the drinks menu that's sitting

on the table.

"Water, please," I say.

The waitress raises her eyebrows and makes a note on her pad.

"I'm assuming you'll have your usual?" Miss Flirty winks at Levi.

"Yes, please." Levi smiles.

The waitress saunters away, and I can't help watching her path to the bar.

When I look back at Levi my mouth is hanging open. "She was flirting with you."

"No she wasn't." He leans back, and puts his arm along the top of the booth.

I scoff, and clench my fingers under the table. "You're blind then."

Levi sits forward and leans his forearms on the table. "She's doing her job."

I glance in the direction of the bar, and see Miss Flirty doing exactly what she did with Levi to another customer. My shoulders loosen. I don't feel so uptight about it now. When I look at Levi again, he's staring at me. Heat creeps into my cheeks.

I realise how this must look to him. I'm jealous of another girl looking at him. Is that what this feeling is? Jealousy? I wasn't prepared for the way her flirting has made me feel, but at least it seems like she does it with all the male customers. Knowing Levi probably isn't special to her makes me feel better. Still, Miss Flirty ogles him again when she brings our drinks.

"She checked you out again," I say.

"Katie, would you relax?" He picks up his beer and

takes a sip. "Can we just have some fun?"

I lean forward and take a sip of my water. "Sure. I can do fun."

Our meals arrive, and I'm grateful this time that Levi doesn't take his eyes from mine.

We chat over our dinner. Levi tells me about this great nightclub they've been going to, and I describe the resort pool at the hotel. Levi orders another beer, and I take a deep breath to stop myself from saying anything. I'm not his mum, so I can't, and shouldn't, tell him what to do.

After that, he orders another, and another. I stick to water, and listen as his words start to slur. He's full of energy though, and he looks so happy. When he goes to the bathroom I take my phone out to check the time. Ten pm. The pub is pretty much full, and the noise level has risen to above comfortable. I want to leave, but I can't do that until Levi comes back.

"Katie. How are you?" Geoff slides into the booth beside me.

By the time I look at him, Jarred and Josephine are seated across from me, a beer in each of their hands. Veronica stands at the end of the table.

"I'm great, thanks," I say.

I don't want to spend the rest of the night with them around, and I crane my neck to see if Levi is coming back from the bathroom.

"Where's Levi?" Veronica asks.

"Here," he says, nudging her shoulder with his.

He has another drink in his hand.

"Nice dinner?" Jarred looks from me to Levi.

"Yeah, great," I say, turning to Geoff. "Could you move,

please?"

He stands, and I shuffle along the seat to get out of the booth.

"Where are you going?" Levi asks.

"Thank you for dinner," I say. "But I'm going to head back."

"Is something wrong?"

I press my lips together. "I'm tired is all. I'll catch up with you later."

"Let me walk you." He sets his drink on the table.

"No, it's fine." I turn and make my way through the crowded pub as quickly as I can, hoping Levi doesn't follow me.

I'm not in the mood to spend time with his friends when I thought I was spending time with him. And I also don't want to be having a conversation with him when he might not remember it tomorrow.

Why does he have to drink? Why can't he just have dinner with me?

I step out into the fresh night air and take a deep breath. It was really claustrophobic inside the pub.

A hand touches my shoulder, and I stop.

"Katie," Levi says. "Why are you going?"

I shrug away from his touch and face him. "I told you, I'm tired. I'll see you later."

But when I try to leave, Levi darts around in front of me, so I stop again. We're in the middle of the mall with the noise from the pub behind me.

"Please stay," Levi says.

"Why? So I can watch you drink yourself stupid?" I snap.

The surprise on his face makes me regret my words.

Nothing

Levi takes a step back. "I've only had a few."

I close my eyes for a second and collect myself so I don't say anything else too mean. "We should talk tomorrow. When you're sober."

"We can talk now." Levi crosses his arms over his chest, and I'm surprised he's so coordinated after the number of beers he's had.

"No, really," I say. "We'll talk about it tomorrow."

"Well, I want to talk now."

"Please move." I look up at Levi, but when I go to step around him he steps in my path again. Anger fills the pit of my stomach and rises into my chest. "Get out of my way, Levi."

"No. I want to talk. Something is bothering you."

I glare at him. The middle of a busy mall is not where I want to be discussing this.

"Fine," I say. "I thought you were taking me out to dinner so we could spend some time together, but instead … You're drunk. And then your friends showed up. It's not my idea of a romantic night. So excuse me again, and move."

"I'm not drunk," he says, like that explains everything.

I blink a few times in an attempt to control my anger. "Has drinking become so normal to you that you can't even see what you're doing to yourself?"

"It's just a few beers, Katie."

"A few too many."

"I'm fine."

"I bet Mason thought exactly the same thing." The words are out before I can stop myself.

The way Levi's brow pinches and his mouth puckers

tells me I've stepped over the line. But right now, I don't care. Maybe he needs to hear the cold hard truth.

"Don't you dare bring him into it," Levi says, clenching his fists. "This is not the same."

"It's exactly the same!" I yell, tears pricking my eyes. My chest heaves as I try to breathe. "You forget, I was there, too. I went through the pain, and the loss, and the heartache, just like you did. I don't want to go through that again."

He shakes his head. "You don't know …"

"I do know. I know I couldn't stop crying for a month after Mason died. And I know it opened a hole in my chest so wide I never thought it would close. But the worst part was, you shut me out. I love you, Levi. And I'm so close to forgiving you for everything you've put me through. But what's the point if all you're going to do is drink yourself stupid all the time? One day, you'll end up right where your brother did, wrapped around a telegraph pole." I stop and swipe the tears from my cheeks. "I can't watch you do this."

"Katie …" Levi reaches for me, but I step back.

"No," I say. "You can't keep doing what you're doing. And if you do, I won't stick around. It's me or the booze. If you want me to stay, you have to choose."

12

The mess I'm in

Karen knew something was wrong the moment I walked into our hotel room. I told her everything. How he's been drinking a lot since he started talking to me again. Or maybe he's been doing it longer than that, and I haven't noticed. How he let me walk away once I delivered my ultimatum. We speculated about a lot of things, and in the end I told her I was tired and wanted to go to bed, because I didn't want to think about it anymore.

Now, it's almost the end of our last day of holidays, and I feel like I haven't had a break from anything.

I dig my toes into the sand, and stare out at the ocean. I came down to the quiet end of the beach, hoping the sound of the waves might calm me, but they haven't.

I'm tired of being on a merry-go-round. I don't know how I should act or feel when I'm around Levi, and it's tearing me apart. One minute everything is perfect, and he's perfect, but then everything changes in an instant.

Is it me?

Am I the one to blame?

Am I asking too much of him?

Or am I overthinking everything?

Last night was the most we've talked about Mason ever, and I accused Levi of being exactly like his brother.

I'm so scared that he'll do something stupid as well.

Today has been hard, because I want Levi to call me so badly, but it's late afternoon and he hasn't. I want to call him, but that would be like saying he doesn't need to be responsible for his actions. If I call and apologise for what I said, where will that leave us?

Right back where we started.

I want to hear his voice, but I also want him to realise he can't keep drinking like he does.

It will destroy him.

It will destroy me.

"Hey." Karen flops onto the sand beside me.

I pull my knees to my chest and hug them. "Hey."

"Feeling any better?"

"I'm ... I don't know."

Karen tucks my hair behind my ear. "Why don't we go out tonight? It's our last night. We can go dancing. You know how much Stacey loves dancing."

I shrug. "Okay."

"We can go to the nightclub Jess and Stacey told us about," Karen says, getting to her feet. "I can't believe you're eighteen, and we haven't gone to a club together yet."

I look up at her. "Sounds noisy."

Nothing

"Come on, Katie." She grabs my hand and pulls me up. "You need to let your hair down. Let's go get ready." She tugs me up the beach towards the road.

We walk the five minutes back to the hotel. Jessica and Stacey are already getting ready for one more night out before going home. While Karen does her makeup, I put on the clothes she suggests, slipping into skinny jeans and a black halter top. Then I go through the trauma of putting my contacts in. Even after all the months I've been wearing them, I still can't seem to do it easily. Still, I like the way I look without my glasses. I don't wear a lot of makeup though, so I just use my usual gloss on my lips, and run a brush through my hair.

"Ready," I say, slipping my feet into my sandals.

Karen grins and grabs her room key from the table. "Let's go have some fun."

"Who said fun?" Stacey asks from the hallway.

"I said fun." Karen pulls our room door closed behind us.

Jessica smiles, but doesn't show as much excitement as the other two. We head downstairs and onto the street.

"It's early," Stacey says, turning her face to the darkening sky. "Dinner first?" She looks at us over her shoulder as we walk.

"Sounds perfect," Karen says. "We can go to the pancake place in the mall."

"For dinner?" I ask. We stop at the lights and wait for them to change.

"I think pancakes for dinner sounds awesome," Jessica says.

We laugh and cross the road, walking towards the

mall with a steady stream of other people. I look around at my friends and feel a moment of gratitude towards them. I'm so lucky to have these three girls in my life. I'm not sure I'd be able to get through any day, let alone every day, if I didn't have them. I want to hug them all.

I settle for slipping my arm through Karen's and giving it a squeeze. Jessica and Stacey walk ahead.

"Everything good?" Karen asks, glancing at me sideways.

I lean my head towards her. "Yeah. I have you."

"Always." She smiles.

When we reach the pancake place it's already pretty full, but they squeeze the four of us onto the end of a long table. It's informal dining, and none of us mind. The atmosphere is full of happy energy. Maybe it has something to do with the sugar everyone is eating.

We each order something different so we can try as much of the menu as possible. Traditional pancakes with maple syrup, pancakes with berries and ice cream, waffles with chocolate and strawberries, and a banana crepe, plus milkshakes all round.

I enjoy a couple of hours with my friends, eating, laughing, and talking about what we plan to do when we get home.

"I would love to take a year off," Jessica says. "Maybe do some travel with Josie? She's pretty excited about it actually. We just have to convince Mum and Dad."

"I think everyone wants a gap year." Karen takes a sip of her milkshake.

"We don't always get what we want," I say.

"I don't think they're a good idea," Stacey says. "You end up a year behind. I think I'd rather get my degree out of the way, then have a year off while I decide if I want to use it or not."

I sip my milkshake. "Why wouldn't you use it?"

Stacey shrugs. "Right now, I want to go into vet science. But in four years' time I might hate animals."

"There's no way you'd ever hate animals," Jessica says.

"Anything can happen."

I look around at my friends. Yes, anything can happen. We don't know what the future holds, but that's what makes it so scary, and, according to Karen, fun at the same time.

I'm suddenly aware of how much time I've wasted this week moping about when I should have been making the most of every second I have with my friends. Who knows where we'll end up next year? What if I've ignored the most important time of our lives together?

"We should go," I say. "There's a dance floor waiting for us."

Karen jumps up. "I think you're right."

Jessica and Stacey get to their feet, and I smile at everyone's enthusiasm. This is what I want. To see my friends happy, and to share that happiness with them. I've been so wrapped up in Levi that I forgot how good I have it. How lucky I am to have these girls in my life.

We pay for our meals at the counter on the way out and head up the mall towards the nightclub. The entrance is via a flight of steps leading to an upper level. We all get carded on the way in.

As soon as we pass through the doors the noise level rises. Lights strobe around the club in blue, pink, and green. A smoky haze floats above the large room. We move farther in towards the bar. Music pumps, and the bass vibrates through my feet. People move violently around the dance floor. The dancing here is nothing like it was at the formal. Stacey's face lights up, and she cranes her neck to get a better look at the dance floor. Karen pulls herself up onto a stool at the bar, and I take the one next to her.

"Come on." Stacey tugs Jessica's hand and leads her through the crowd towards the dance floor.

Karen and I laugh, and watch with smiles on our faces.

"Drink?" she yells in my ear.

I nod. Karen picks up the cocktail list and raises her eyebrows. I hesitate, but then nod again. I'll only have one. I'm not going to drink to get drunk. I just want to enjoy a night with my girlfriends.

Karen orders two Pina Coladas, and the bartender asks us for ID, even though we were asked at the door. I don't mind, and I smile when I hand him my licence. He winks at me before making our drinks.

I sip my cocktail and scan the crowd, watching Stacey and Jessica on the dance floor, and checking out what some of the girls are wearing. Their outfits make my jeans and halter top look like rags.

Karen and I sit like that for another two rounds. Every now and then, she points and I smile or laugh. Or the other way around. I'm surprised at how easily the cocktails go down, and a nice buzz courses through me. I feel happy.

Someone sits on the bar stool beside me, but I don't pay them any attention.

The person leans over and yells in my ear, "You can't stay away from me, can you?"

Nothing

I turn to see Scott, the guy I met on the beach who tried to force himself on me. Seems like my knee to his crotch wasn't obvious enough. I stiffen, smile with my lips closed, and then angle my body away from him and towards Karen, taking another sip of my cocktail. We're in a crowded nightclub and Karen is right next to me. Surely Scott won't touch me here.

Scott moves to stand in front of us. "Would you ladies like a drink?"

I hold up my glass and raise my eyebrows. "Already have one." But I don't know if he can hear me.

"Who is this guy?" Karen yells at me over the music.

I crinkle my nose, and lean close to her ear. "Met him on the beach. He's a creep."

I never told Karen what happened that night. If she knew, she'd be kneeing him in the balls right now, harder than I did.

Karen looks him up and down. "Yeah, I'll have a drink."

I glare at her and hope she gets my 'What the hell are you doing?' vibe.

Scott grins, and I turn away, cringing. I finish my cocktail, but I don't think accepting a drink from him is a good idea. Still, I go with the flow, keeping an eye on Scott and the glasses to make sure he doesn't spike them with something. Scott hands us a vodka and orange each. I sip the sweet drink through the straw, not sure if I like the taste of it after three Pina Coladas. I take another few sips, then set my glass on the bar.

I lean over and put my lips to Karen's ear. "Let's dance."

She sucks half her drink through the straw, then jumps down from the bar stool. I link my fingers through hers, and follow her through the crowd to the pulsating mass of bodies on the dance floor. It takes us a few moments, but we spot Stacey and Jessica a few people in, swinging their hips, and waving their hands like everyone else.

Karen and I join them, and it takes five minutes of dancing for me to be grateful I wore flat shoes. The lights strobe around us, and I lose myself in the rhythm of the music, moving to the beat and concentrating on nothing but how it makes me feel. I'm buzzing from head to toe, and I figure it's the alcohol, but I don't care. The power of the bass beats through my body, and I forget about everything that's happened.

It feels good.

Hands touch my waist, and someone presses up against my back. I turn to see Scott behind me, and my happy moment is ruined. In my frantic attempt to get away from him, I stumble into the people beside me, and a girl falls to the ground.

"I'm so sorry," I yell, but my voice is drowned out.

I reach down to help her to her feet, aware that someone's hand is on my arse. Once the girl is up, I turn again and confront Scott. I want to scream at him but there's no point. He won't be able to hear me, so I'd be wasting my breath. He grins at me.

I push my way off the dance floor.

I can't breathe. It's too stuffy in here.

I make it as far as the bar, and my head spins. I grab a stool to steady myself. The barman smirks then pours a glass of water and pushes it towards me. I sit on the stool and take the glass, downing the cool liquid in three gulps.

Nothing

"What the hell happened?" Stacey yells in my ear.

"Are you all right?" Jessica grabs my arm.

Karen pulls me to my feet. "Let's get out of here. You need some air."

My friends surround me, and we shuffle towards the exit. I stumble going down the stairs and into the mall. The cool night air hits my face, and I break out in a sweat. A sick feeling creeps into my stomach. I'm not sure if it's from the alcohol or having Scott's grubby hands on me again. It's probably a combination of both.

I concentrate on the sound of the waves crashing on the beach across the road—anything to take my mind off the way that creep looked at me. The way he touched me, tonight and the other night on the beach ... My hand goes to my throat.

"Let's sit down," Karen says. She leads us to the pedestrian crossing, and we make our way over to the beach side of the strip. The four of us head to the steps and sit on the top few. I stare out at the dark ocean and take slow breaths, trying to get the sick feeling in my stomach to settle down.

"What did that guy do to you?" Stacey asks.

I grimace and turn my face towards her. "He grabbed me."

"Looked like he wanted to dance with you." Jessica tucks her hair behind her ear.

"He bought us a drink while you guys were on the dance floor," Karen says. "I think he wanted more than a dance."

"You're right." I take a deep breath and stare at my hands. "Our first night here, when I stayed on the beach—"

"When you were late, and I was about to come look for you?" Karen asks.

I nod, my stomach rolling. I swallow before continuing. "That guy ... Scott. He came over and talked to me. He asked me to come to this party they were having near the steps that lead to the sand. I said no, but then I saw Veronica and she called me over." I shrug. "I went to talk to her, then Scott saw me and introduced me to his friends. After I left to come back to the hotel, he followed me. The beach was dark. He ... grabbed me."

"That bastard," Stacey says.

I offer her a small smile. "I gave him a good knee in the balls."

"Go you," Karen says.

My friends laugh, and I do, too, but it's not funny, and I still feel sick.

"I'm not sure I would've gotten away from him if it wasn't for Geoff," I say.

"Geoff?" Karen asks. "Geoff Wilcox?"

"It's ironic really." I look at her. "Geoff is ..."

"Yeah. He's a dick. What he did to Veronica ..." Karen stops. Her eyes go wide, and her hand flies to her mouth.

"What did he do to Veronica?" Stacey stands up.

I shake my head. "We promised her we wouldn't tell." I glare at Karen.

"No, you can't do that. You can't say something then not tell us," Stacey says.

"I know about it." Jessica stares out at the beach.

"What?" Karen and Stacey say at the same time.

I put my face in my hands. I'm not surprised. Josephine and Veronica are friends. Josephine probably told Jessica at some stage.

"She asked us not to tell anyone, okay?" I say. "Just … let it go. And to Geoff's credit, if he didn't turn up, who knows what Scott would've done to me."

"You should report him," Karen says.

I shrug. "I told Veronica the same thing."

"And did she?"

"I don't think so." I look at Karen. "There's no point. I'll never see him again, and he didn't … I got away."

We all go quiet. Stacey frowns, then walks down a few steps and leans against the stair railing, crossing her arms over her chest. Karen bites her lip and stares at her feet. Jessica puts her arm around my shoulders and gives me a gentle hug. I concentrate on not throwing up, swallowing a few times to suppress the urge. My head spins, and I think now it's definitely the alcohol.

There are a few people about, walking into and out of the mall, and hanging out on the beach. Murmuring voices float on the air, mingling with the crashing waves. Cars pass on the road. The traffic lights behind us tick as they change.

"There she is," someone says.

Feet shuffle behind us. I look over my shoulder towards the voice. Scott stops a few metres away from the steps, and he's brought friends. My head pounds, but I recognise the other boys from the beach earlier in the week.

I get to my feet, swaying a little, and face the three boys. Jessica gets up as well, and she and Stacey move to my side.

Karen steps forward. "You touch her again and I'll hurt you."

Scott laughs. "Wow, Katie. Your friend is feisty." He stares at me, and it makes my skin crawl. "We just want to buy you a few more drinks."

"Yeah." One of the boys grins. "Why don't you come back to the club and show us a good time?"

"Because you putting your hands where they're not wanted isn't our idea of a good time," Karen says. "Go find someone else to have *fun* with." She makes quote marks in the air with her fingers. "Or I'll call the cops."

"You do that." Scott raises his chin.

The three boys come towards us. Karen stands her ground, but Stacey and Jessica pull me down the stairs until we're standing on the halfway platform. My knees are weak, and it's getting harder to stop myself from being sick.

Scott puts his hands up. "I'm sorry about that, really. Can we start over?" He smiles at me, and my stomach rolls.

Jessica and Stacey are still beside me, so close I can hear them breathing.

"He looks like a creep," Stacey whispers in my ear.

Scott shoulders past Karen and comes down the stairs. His two mates stay at the top.

Karen looks up and down the street before following. "Get away from them."

"I want to talk to Katie." Scott stops in front of me. "I really like you. I'm sorry if I went about it the wrong way. The other night ... I was a drunken idiot. Can we take a walk and maybe chat?" He angles his head down and stares at me through his lashes, giving me a look I'm pretty sure he thinks is going to win me over.

"I don't want to talk to you," I say, swaying. I have to

blink a few times to see him properly. "Didn't you get the message when I kneed you in the balls?"

He comes closer, still smiling, and then I vomit all over him.

"You bitch," Scott yells.

I'm off the ground and over his shoulder.

Stacey cries out and stumbles on the steps.

"Katie!" Karen yells.

Bitterness fills my mouth. The taste makes me gag. I kick my legs and pummel Scott's back with my fists, but he doesn't let go. When his feet hit the sand he stumbles, his shoulder digging into my stomach. Karen, Jessica, and Stacey yell but I can't see them. Their voices blur into one frantic sound. Scott's shoulder digs into my stomach as he runs, and more bile rises into my throat. A siren wails on the strip, and I catch a glimpse of red and blue lights.

The waves crashing on the shore get louder. Scott stops and drops me. I hit the water and the cold envelopes me, filling my mouth and my nose. When I come up I cough and splutter, flopping around in the shallows as I try to get to my feet. Then I'm plunged under again, a hand forcing my head down. *Scott's hand?* His fingers curl into my hair and yank me up. I cough again, my arms flailing as I try to grab onto something.

"Hey, what are you doing?" I hear Levi's voice.

The hand releases my hair, and I fall to my knees in the shallows. I try to turn towards Levi, but pain shoots into my head and the world spins.

"None of your business," I hear Scott say. I don't know where he's gone.

Then he grabs my arm. His fingers dig into my skin.

"Get off her," Levi yells.

Where is he?

More voices shout around me, but I can't make out the words.

I scramble on the sand on my hands and knees. The water rushes over my legs as the tide comes in. I look up as Levi's fist connects with Scott's face. I vomit again, then fall onto the sand and roll until I'm looking at the sky. The twinkling stars remind me of the stickers on my bedroom ceiling, and I wonder how the hell I got myself into the mess I'm in.

The chance to begin

I open my eyes. Sunlight sears my retinas, so I squeeze them shut again. There's a dull ache in my head, and when I lift it, a sharp pain pierces my temple. I wince as I try to sit up, but everything hurts, so I resort to rolling onto my side.

"Hey, sleepyhead," Levi says.

I open my eyes to slits. He's sitting on the floor beside my bed, leaning against the wall with his knees pulled up. There's a bucket between us with a face washer draped over the lip.

"What are you doing here?" I groan. "What happened?"

"You got drunk."

"I tried to make him leave." Karen leans out of the bathroom doorway. "But he wouldn't go away. He's been here all night."

Levi chuckles. "I take it you're not feeling so good."

"Like someone has scooped my brain out with a spoon." I groan again, and cover my eyes with my hand.

"Do you still feel sick?" Karen asks.

I peek at her through my fingers. "I don't think so. But I haven't stood up yet. How many times did I ... was I sick?"

"Before or after you upchucked all over Scott?" Karen raises her eyebrows and grins.

I move my hand to my mouth. "Oh ... that happened, didn't it?"

Last night comes back to me in a huge tidal wave. Drinking cocktails. The vodka Scott bought us. Dancing. Scott grabbing me. He and his friends following us. Me vomiting all over him. Then him trying to drown me in the ocean. Levi clocking him one in the jaw. The police showed up after that. Apparently, they'd been looking for Scott, and I wasn't the first girl he'd assaulted. They questioned all of us. I refused to go anywhere but back to the hotel, so they told Karen to get me to bed.

"He deserved it," Karen yells from the bathroom.

"He also deserved my fist in his face." Levi says.

Karen sticks her head out the bathroom door. "It was fun watching the police take him away in the paddy wagon. I'm going to take some stuff to the car."

"Okay."

She grabs her suitcase and rolls it out to the hall. We're going home today, but the last thing I feel like doing is sitting in a car for hours. I wish we could fly home, so I could be in my own bed tonight.

The door clicks closed.

Nothing

Levi clears his throat. "My flight's in a couple of hours. I should go soon."

I hang my arm over the side of the bed and study him. Levi seeing me like this is really embarrassing, but I don't want him to go.

"Did you have a good break?" I ask.

Levi moves the bucket and gets on his knees, coming to the side of the bed. I move so he can rest his elbows on it, and he's close enough to kiss me. I press my lips together and hope my morning breath isn't too stinky.

"It was okay," he says. Then he frowns. "Katie, I ... I'm really sorry for the way I've behaved." He stares at me. "What you said the other night ... about me having to choose. I choose you."

I smile, but I don't say anything, because I'm not sure if I completely believe him. Is he saying this in a last-ditch effort to win me back? Or does he *really* mean it?

"How can I be sure you mean it?" I ask. "What if we get home, and nothing changes?"

Levi adjusts his position and takes my hand. "After seeing you drunk ... everything has changed. Do I look like that to you?"

My eyes widen. "Oh my God, what did I do?"

Levi chuckles. "You didn't *do* anything, Katie, but you were a bit ... messy." Levi wrinkles his nose. "Am I like that?"

"Mostly you're cocky and obnoxious." Despite the pounding in my head, I prop myself up on my elbow and smile.

"Really?" He laughs again.

"But you're like that when you're sober, too." My smile

widens, and I hope he knows I'm teasing him.

Levi leans forward and presses his forehead to mine. "Katie." He takes a deep breath.

I put my finger on his lips. "Don't. Please don't apologise again. You don't need to. I need to thank you ... If you weren't there last night ..."

"That guy is a right royal dick," Levi says.

"Yep, he is." I close my eyes, and concentrate on the feeling of Levi's skin touching mine.

"Last night," Levi says a few moments later, "I saw you in a way I never have before."

"Yeah. Drunk," I say without looking at him.

"Well ... yeah." He plays with the ends of my hair. "But jokes aside, seriously ... do I look like that? You know ... when I've been drinking?"

I open my eyes and pull away so I can take in Levi's face.

"Look like what?" I ask.

He presses his lips together. "Messy. Out of control. You couldn't talk or walk straight."

"You're acting like you've never seen anyone drunk before."

Levi shakes his head. "That's not it. Seeing you like that, then thinking about how I must look to you ... it made me feel ashamed. I understand now why you get so upset when I'm drunk, and why you don't like it."

I sigh and link my fingers through Levi's. "I *don't* like it. I just wish you'd talk to me instead of trying to hide from everything. But I can't tell you what to do. I can only tell you how your actions make me feel." I move, and wince at the pain in my head. "How do you cope with a hangover? It's horrible." I flop back onto the bed.

Levi gets up on his knees and leans over me. "Katie, you're too good for me."

I stare up at him. "You know I think the same thing about you?"

"When we get home, can we start over?" Levi squeezes my hand. "Can we put everything behind us and … try again?"

He's asking me for a second chance, and I want to give it to him. But how do I know everything is going to be okay? Am I about to set myself up for another fall? But then how amazing would it be if everything worked out?

Pretty amazing.

Maybe I need to take the chance.

"Starting over would be nice," I say.

Levi's lips curl into a smile. I hold my breath, because in a perfect world now would be when he kissed me, and my breath probably stinks.

I want him to kiss me though.

Levi leans down, and brushes my lips with his, then the door bursts open and his touch is gone just as quickly.

"You're still in bed?" Karen asks.

I glare at her. "We were talking."

"Your bags won't pack themselves. Come on. I'll be next door." Karen goes back out to the hall.

Levi and I look at each other, then burst out laughing. I push myself up, and Levi gets to his feet. He holds out his hand and helps me out of bed.

"I need a shower," I say. "Can you wait?"

Levi checks his phone. "Sure. I've got time."

"Great." I tuck my hair behind my ear, and search

through my case for a clean top, shorts, and underwear. "Be right back."

The shower helps to relieve the horrible heavy feeling in my body. I vow never to touch alcohol again. I hope Levi meant it when he said he wanted to start over. We both could use a new beginning, and going home seems like the best place to start.

I smile at my reflection in the mirror, at the thought of spending time with him when we get back. After towelling dry, dressing, and brushing my teeth, I don't bother with my contacts since Karen and I will be in the car half the day. When I come out of the bathroom, Levi is sitting on the bed.

He stands and comes over to me. He takes the wet towel from my hands and throws it on the bed. Then he brushes my cheek with his fingertips. I blink behind my glasses, and stare up at him. He leans down, and I part my lips.

The door to the room opens again.

"Oh my God, you two have the worst timing," Karen says.

I glare at her for the second time this morning. "We have bad timing?"

Karen looks from me to Levi. "Just kiss her already."

I clear my throat. Karen shakes her head, and goes into the bathroom.

When I turn back to Levi, he's staring down at me with a small lopsided smile. "Can I kiss you now?"

I nod, but I don't speak, because if I do my voice will crack.

Levi pulls me close, and I put my arms around his

neck. I bite my lip as he closes the gap between us, and then his lips are on mine, firm but soft. In that kiss I forget about all the fights we've had, and all the stuff that's happened between us. I forget how hard it is to love him sometimes, because right now loving him is the easiest thing in the world. For a few heartbeats, it's just me and Levi. Nothing else.

Levi breaks our kiss. "I should go. Don't want to miss my flight."

"Okay." I'm not sure how I get the word out, because he's taken my breath away.

"You and me ... tomorrow," he says.

"I'll come see you when I get home."

"I'm looking forward to climbing in your window."

"You'll need a ladder." I laugh. "I ripped the lattice down, remember?"

"Shouldn't be a problem." He kisses the tip of my nose.

Levi walks to the door, and I want so badly to pull him back and hug him, but I twist my fingers together and offer him a small smile instead. There will be plenty of time for hugs when we get home.

The door clicks closed with Levi on one side and me on the other, and I let out a long breath. I move around the room to collect all the things that have made their way into various places since we've been away.

"Is it safe to come out?" Karen calls from the bathroom.

I laugh. "Yes, he's gone."

The door opens and Karen smiles. "You almost ready?"

"Yep." I throw the last of my clothes into my suitcase and zip it closed.

We go next door and say goodbye to Jessica and Stacey

before checking out and heading to the hotel car park. Karen and I pack the last of our things into the boot of her mum's car. It's been a long break with so much happening, and I'm glad we're finally heading home. After last night, and my talk this morning with Levi, I think I'm finally ready to forgive him for what he did. Because even after all the things he's done that have hurt me, I know there is nothing he wouldn't do for me if I asked him.

Maybe that's been my problem all along. Maybe all I have to do is tell him exactly how I feel about him, and *ask* him if he feels the same. Maybe I need to stop living in the past and look to the future.

"Ready?" Karen asks, closing the boot of the car.

"Yeah. Let's go home."

We get in and drive out of the hotel car park to navigate the streets of Surfers Paradise. We hit the motorway heading south, and before long we cross the border back into more familiar territory. I wish we could be home tonight, but we have a cabin booked in Coffs Harbour, and I'm looking forward to spending the time with Karen. It will be nice to debrief on the week, especially since I didn't make it all that great for her.

After a quick lunch stop we keep driving, and we make it to Coffs with plenty of time to grab some fish and chips for dinner, and hit the beach at sunset. Even though the sun isn't setting over the water, the sky is still lit with beautiful shades of pink, peach, and gold.

I dig my toes into the sand, and pick at the food sitting on the brown paper between us.

My phone buzzes so I pull it from my pocket. "It's Jess.

She and Stacey got home okay."

Seconds later, Karen's phone trills with a text message. She holds it up so I can see the screen.

"Same message," we both say at the same time, then we laugh.

Karen stares out at the water, and I sigh, happy that my friends are safe, and that I get to be here with my best friend in this moment.

"I'm sorry," I say, stuffing another chip in my mouth.

Karen turns to me. "What the hell for?"

I shrug. "You know … ruining your week."

"You did not." She throws a chip at me. "Don't be stupid."

"Come on. We both know it could've been better."

"Maybe. But it doesn't matter." Karen smiles. "You and Levi made up."

A grin spreads across my face. "Yeah. We did."

"So …" Karen pops a chip in her mouth. "What next?"

"I guess we see what happens. Go with the flow."

It's the best answer I can give her, because I'm not entirely sure about the future. I don't know exactly where I'm heading. But I do know I want Levi, and when I get home that's the first thing I'm going to tell him. I want him, and this time, nothing is going to come between us.

"You've forgiven him then?" Karen asks.

"Forgiveness is an ongoing thing." I dust the salt from my fingers and lean back in the sand. "I'm not sure I'm completely there, but I'm close. And we have to start somewhere."

"Well, I'm here for you whenever you need me."

I smile at my best friend, so grateful that I have her in

my life. We roll up what's left of our dinner and put the parcel in the bin on the way back to our cabin. We're both pretty tired and have another day of driving tomorrow, so we turn in early. I have trouble getting to sleep though, and I lie awake for a while, wishing I was at home staring at the stars on my ceiling.

I lie here and think about the first thing I'm going to say to Levi when I get home. I close my eyes, and when I open them again, it's morning and sunlight is streaming through the window. Karen is making breakfast in the little kitchenette. I roll over and watch her through the door of the tiny bedroom.

"Tea?" she asks, smiling.

"That would be great."

My head doesn't ache this morning like it did yesterday, and getting up isn't as hard. A warm shower wakes me up even more, and I feel pretty great when I get out. I sit at the little table with Karen and towel-dry my hair before downing my tea as quickly as I can.

"In a hurry?" Karen asks.

I bite my lip and get up to put my cup in the sink. "Is it that obvious?"

"It's okay." She laughs. "Summer is officially here, and I want to get home, too."

"Let's go then."

We quickly clean up and pack our stuff into the car. We don't talk much on the drive, and I like that I don't have to fill uncomfortable silences with Karen. We crank the music, so talking is a bit hard anyway. I roll my window down, lean back in my seat, and close my eyes, letting the wind brush my face.

Nothing

It's mid-afternoon by the time we pull off the motorway, and in less than ten minutes I'll be able to go and see Levi. My hairs prickle on my skin, and a shot of excitement runs through me. We're not in school anymore. I don't have to see all the people who have made my life hell for so long every day of the week. I can spend time with Levi without anyone judging us.

We have our whole future ahead of us.

Karen pulls the car up to the kerb outside my house and kills the engine.

"Home sweet home," she says.

I smile. I think we're both happy that schoolies is over and we can resume our normal programming. Karen flings her door open and gets out. I grab my purse and follow, meeting her at the boot of the car.

"Thanks for a great week," I say. "Even if I wasn't so great at times. It was … an experience."

Karen laughs. "It sure was. And I wouldn't have wanted to spend it with anyone else."

She pops the boot and I grab my bags, hoisting my backpack over one shoulder and grabbing the handle of my suitcase.

"Are you going to go see Levi?" Karen nods in the direction of his house.

I shrug and look over to his empty driveway. "Yeah. I guess. Doesn't look like he's home though."

"If he's not, call him. Then call me tomorrow?" Karen gives me a hug, slams the boot, then gets back in the car. "We can go get hot chocolate," she calls through the open window.

"Sounds great." I wave as she drives away, then make

my way to the front door. "I'm home," I say as I push the door open. "Hello?"

Mum and Dad come through from the kitchen.

"Katie, honey. I'm so sorry." Mum wraps me in a hug, and I drop my bags to hug her back.

I pull away. "Sorry about what?"

"We thought you might have heard already."

"Heard what?" I ask with a bit more force.

Mum presses her lips together and glances at Dad. Her eyes sparkle with tears.

"I'm sorry," she says again. "There's been an accident."

I stare at her. "What do you mean? What's happened?"

"Maybe you should sit down." Dad takes me by the elbow.

I pull away from his grasp and step back, my heart racing. "I don't want to sit down. Tell me what's going on."

Mum and Dad exchange another glance.

"It's Levi," Mum says. "He's in the hospital."

"It doesn't look good." Dad steps towards me.

Mum presses her lips into a thin line. "It's too early to tell if he'll make it."

I move away from them again, and my back hits the front door. My fingers tighten on the purse in my hand. Blood rushes to my ears and my heart pounds. *Hospital? Accident? What kind of accident? What do they mean, if he'll make it?* I want to ask my parents these questions, and so many more, but when I open my mouth, no sound comes out.

I shake my head. My hands go numb. This can't be happening.

Nothing

"No," I whisper.

Levi is in the hospital?

He can't be. I'm ready to tell him I forgive him. Starting from now, we're supposed to have our entire future ahead of us, but what if he doesn't make it?

I can't lose him.

I love him.

My heart breaks at the thought that I may not be able to tell him.

Are we over before we've had the chance to begin?

Katie's story concludes in …

Everything

All the Things: part three

Acknowledgements

*F*irst thanks go to Selina Fenech and Serene Conneeley. This book wouldn't be where it is now without your amazing help and support. Thank you for the encouraging talks, the wine and tea, for not making speeches, and just believing in me.

To my wonderfully patient and supportive husband, Brendon, I promise you can read it when I'm finished, so stop looking over my shoulder.

Thank you, Emily and Jayden, for reminding me what life is about when I'm lost in my own imagination. You both keep me grounded when I need it most.

To the countless people I interact with on a daily basis in the online self-publishing community. Thank you, your stories and advice do not go unnoticed. I'm very grateful to be a part of the indie network.

To my editor, Lauren Clarke, thank you for your all-round awesomeness.

And to my readers, I hope you enjoyed the second part of Katie's story.

About the author

K. A. Last was born in Subiaco, Western Australia, and moved to Sydney when she was eight. Artistic and creative by nature, she studied Graphic Design and graduated with an Advanced Diploma. After marrying her high school sweetheart, she concentrated on her career before settling into family life. Blessed with a vivid imagination, K. A. Last began writing to let off creative steam, and fell in love with it. She is currently studying her Bachelor of Arts at Charles Sturt University, with a major in English, and minors in Children's Literature, Art History, and Visual Culture. She now resides in the countryside on the mid-north coast of NSW with her family and a menagerie of animals.

Connect with K. A. Last

Website www.kalastbooks.com.au
Facebook www.facebook.com/KALastBooks
Instagram www.instagram.com/kalastbooks
Pinterest www.pinterest.com/kalast
Goodreads www.goodreads.com/KALast
Twitter www.twitter.com/KALastBooks

**Scan the code to subscribe to
K. A. Last's newsletter.**

Available Now

Is love really worth the fall?

THE TATE CHRONICLES

Scan for more information

Available Now

**Do you have a story idea
but don't know how to start writing?**

A Novel Idea! combines the therapeutic art of colouring
with the craft of creative writing, and provides you
with all the prompts needed to help turn your initial
light bulb moment into something special.